The Drowning
The Dancing

The Drowning
The Dancing

by Jerome Nilssen

FORTRESS PRESS   PHILADELPHIA

To

THE PEOPLE OF DANEBOD

Contents

April 12, 1963

(From the Diary of Pfc. Paul Westfield)

I don't know how they do it now, but not so many years ago the slaughterhouses killed cattle by knocking them on the forehead with a sledge hammer. They were huge men who did the killing, and they never seemed to miss or even strike a glancing blow. They aimed, swung up, and crashed down between and a few inches above the eyes. You heard a muffled, hollow sound, and the poor beast would stand there a minute appearing very confused, as if he could not really believe he was dead. Next he would shuffle forward maybe half a step, and then he would topple over, actually onto a conveyor belt that carried him along to be stripped of his hide and butchered.

I said he stood for a minute. It was probably only a matter of seconds after he was hit that he fell. But when you watched it as an outsider it *felt* like a longer time. In fact, it felt like such a long time that it seemed a cruel way to kill. Of course, the people in the slaughterhouses said that it wasn't, but they never entirely convinced me, particularly when they also said that the men who do the killing have to be shifted to other jobs periodically. They gave no reasons, they just stated it as the way things were. I suspect, though, that it had something to do with a lust for killing. I mean, some, and maybe most, of the men

1

may have had an initial repulsion against this kind of slaughter for the first six or dozen deaths. But then the routine set in, and swinging the sledge became a job like any other job. And finally, after the routine became rhythm, there may have developed a subliminal fascination for generating death so smoothly and efficiently, and perhaps even a desire to speed up the process, to become even more fluid and efficient.

But this is all speculation, beside the point. It might lead you to suspect me of being sentimental, too. But as a soldier who is now being trained to kill, who has swung a rifle butt hard across a canvas bag with the "face" of this year's enemy stenciled on it, then reflected for a split second, I am not very well equipped for crusades against cruelty to animals. I only now put into words (not because it is original with me, but because it is necessary for me to remember) what I reflected for a split second: The killer can only kill once; the victim, human or animal, possesses the last, actually the more durable, irony— he can take away his murderer's humanity. What I would like to say is that when he died we reacted like those sledge-struck cattle. We heard the news and we just stood there like poor dumb beasts who had suddenly been killed and didn't really know it or believe it.

But it is just as true, maybe more true, that we reacted like the killers of the beasts: so accustomed to news of violence and sudden, senseless death, so unaccustomed to genuine passion, that we really felt nothing at all . . . except, perhaps, a mild embarrassment and a general desire to drop the whole subject, to forget—the sooner the better. I mean, there was no place for us to move to, like they moved the cattle killers, so naturally we had to forget, to return as quickly as possible to business as usual. After all, there are certain things, certain acts, that a community has got to bury deep down, or else the community won't be able to live normally. And still, in some circumstances, that might be the biggest sin of all: to try to live normally, on an even keel, to pretend that nothing can ever shatter the way we've always thought and done things.

His name was Jesse Christian. I don't know how he got his last name. I have heard of Christian as a first name, but never before as a last name (although there are many things that are true despite my not knowing about them). But he might have made it up, too, because he wasn't beyond making things up. It isn't that he told lies; he told stories.

So when I asked him once about his last name he told me instead about a man who had come down from Arkansas into a small town in West Texas. The man took a job in a restaurant washing dishes, and when people asked him about his name he said it was Lazarus.

"You can't have a name like that," the people said to him.

"Yes, I can," he answered. "My name is Lazarus because God gave me that name. He said to me, 'You are Lazarus; go and tell the people that.' "

But this only made the people angry, and either they ignored him or they intentionally and obscenely mispronounced his name. Then one day one of the men who ate regularly in the restaurant mentioned to a friend sitting next to him that Lazarus had uncommonly large ears and a sharp nose. "He looks sort of like a mouse, doesn't he?" said the man.

"He looks like Mickey Mouse," said the other.

And from that time on everyone called him Mickey, or Mick. At first Lazarus did not respond to his new name.

3

But it was not too long before the silence and the lone-liness became more oppressive than he could bear. Then, standing before the man who had given him his new name, he said, "All right, my name is Mickey; call me Mickey." Everyone in the restaurant laughed, and the name-giver held out his hand as if to confirm the new name. But the next day Mickey, whose name was once Lazarus, disappeared, and he was never seen again.

I suppose I heard Jesse Christian tell this story at least three different times, each time when someone asked him about his name. But he never said anything about his own name, whether it really was his own. Instead he told stories.

However, all this is not getting his story told, which is what I have set out to do. In the first place, our town is Nortonville, located in western Minnesota on the shore of Spider Lake, the tenth biggest in the state. I think we have a good community, people who are generally hard-working and honest. There are some exceptions who drink too much too often or commit senseless acts of vandalism such as knocking over the tall granite monument on the edge of town, the one that proclaims Nortonville "The Pheasant Capital of the World." But I am still proud of my town, and I will never do as some Nortonvillites who, when they are out of the state, tell people they are from Minneapolis, which everybody has heard of, instead of Nortonville, which has only forty-eight hundred inhab-itants and is not exactly famous, even though there is ex-cellent fishing on the lake year round and there are quite a few game birds in the fall.

Anyway, as you can imagine, we can spot a stranger when he moves into town, since it is hardly big enough to hide in, particularly not big enough for a Negro—which is what Jesse Christian was—to hide in. This bothered a lot of people, who wondered what he was looking for, worried about what he wanted. Too self-contained, self-possessed to be "our nigger," he was more like an exclamation point, stopping, seizing. It didn't help that he was a bona fide landowner, either. This made him permanent. We had had Negroes come through before, to fish or to hunt. We had even had Negroes working in the local canning company for a whole summer, and they had never caused any trouble, either. But here was one who let us know very plainly that he planned to stay.

For most of the people this meant, for better or worse, simply trying to forget about him, keeping their eyes—or their minds—closed. But there was at least one exception: Jesse Christian's neighbor to the south, Tony Sauer. Tony is a man I happen to appreciate, since he taught me all I know about fishing, especially bass fishing, so I do not intend to make any judgments about the man one way or the other, although I will state that he probably likes liquor a little more than is good for him. Nevertheless, I am no one to condemn a man for his weaknesses, since we all have our share.

Tony owns a lakeshore resort about two miles north of the city limits. It's not a very modern resort, but he manages to keep it full most of the summer with families from Nebraska and South Dakota who have never before seen any more water in one place than you can run into a stock tank. His cabins rent for only five or six dollars a day, and he always tells his guests where they'll be sure to catch fish. He also takes time to show them what bait to use and how to cast and how far down to let the line sink, and they like that attention, and if they don't come back the next year a lot of them send their neighbors. Anybody

5

from Minneapolis or the resort country farther north would laugh at the kind of place Tony runs—he doesn't even have indoor plumbing—but if you were from Nebraska or South Dakota, out on the plains where the dust in the cattle yard gets ankle-deep in July and August, it could be a pretty welcome sight.

Jesse Christian had forty acres just north of Sauer's. One of the first things he did after he moved in, Tony told me later, was to tell Tony that the people staying at the resort were welcome to use his beach any time they wanted to.

And in turn Tony helped Jesse around his place, cleaning up, painting, shingling the house, and patching up the old barn where Jesse kept a cow, some sheep, and chickens. The house had been owned for years by the two Larson brothers, the oldest of seven children who had been raised in the house. One by one the others finished high school and moved away, and the parents died, and finally Albert and Clarence were left all alone. As the years went by they kept more and more to themselves, and they let the place run down. They died—I suppose they were both in their seventies—on the same night: Albert had a heart attack and Clarence shot himself through the heart. No one will ever know which came first, the attack or the shot. Either way, the one who went first was too tired to live any longer, and the one left was too frightened to stay on by himself.

After that happened, nobody around Nortonville was too anxious to buy the place. It was too small to farm, the barn was not much good, the house was old and crammed with junk and dirt, and, of course, even though the blood was scrubbed out, people remembered. But then one day Jesse Christian appeared in town with the deed. The house had been advertised in the Minneapolis and Des Moines papers by the Larsons' younger sister, and Jesse bought it from her. At least that's what he told Tony, and that's what Tony told me.

It is not at all surprising, really, that Tony and Jesse became good friends, since Tony was an outsider, too. He was originally from Detroit and, so everybody said, had worked as a bootlegger during prohibition days. In fact, some people say that when he left Detroit and came to Nortonville, around 1939, it was because he had double-crossed the syndicate. All I know is what I have heard: that he had enough money to pay cash for the land and the house he lives in, and enough left over to build the seven log cabins that make up the resort. That was a long time ago, but people have long memories about some things, so Tony has always been viewed somewhat as a gangster. This is pretty ridiculous, when you look at Tony: about five and a half feet tall; bald, with a fringe around the sides like an old monk; fat and red-nosed from too much beer; a permanent squint from looking over the lake into the afternoon sun; corduroy pants and a red lumberjack shirt and boots that lace up almost to his knees. He always speaks, even on dry land, in a soft whispery voice, in order not to frighten away the fish.

I imagine, then, that it was a considerable relief to many when they saw how well Jesse and Tony got along—the gangster and the Negro. They soon became known as "that pair," not because they were often seen together or because they spent a great deal of time together, but because they just seemed to belong together; they made sense as a pair, while individually they stuck out, they intruded. It meant that their relationship could be an occasional source for idle gossip, without threat of involvement.

Maybe the best way I can explain it—the way it was between the townspeople and Jesse and Tony—is to describe the time Jesse's barn burned down. I was fourteen at the time; Jesse Christian had been living on the Larson place about a year, long enough so that the house and barn were in fairly good shape again and long enough so that people had begun to talk about "that colored fellow's place" instead of "the old Larson place." It was before, but not much before, they talked about "out around Tony and Jesse's."

During this time it was primarily the adults who talked about Jesse Christian; in school, his name was hardly ever mentioned, except by the Willson twins, Don and Dale. They were seniors, and they lived on the Point, a peninsula that jutted into the lake like a scythe and covered roughly thirty or forty acres. The Point was five miles up the lake from Jesse's; it hooked down, so that at the very tip of the Point you could see Jesse's land and the whole lakeshore right into Nortonville. Howard Willson, the twins' father, bought the land in 1945 when he got out of the army, and then he built a resort. But it isn't at all like Tony's; it's modern, and there is a pavilion built on stilts over the water with a restaurant and a bar and a dance floor. And on weekends some peole drive as far as a hundred miles just to eat there and dance to live music. There are a lodge, with around forty rooms, and twenty cabins, all winterized. Outside, the lodge and the cabins look very plain and rustic; inside, the rooms are very elegant, with wall-to-wall carpeting and air conditioning and television.

So it isn't very hard to guess who has the best business and makes the most money. This has never bothered Tony. But it has always bothered Howard Willson to have Tony

only a few miles away. Tony's guests couldn't afford to
stay at the Point, so Tony has never exactly been competi-
tion for Mr. Willson. Still, Howard Willson used to report
Tony continually to the state fire marshal and the game
warden and the insurance investigators and the health in-
spectors. My father, who is a good friend of the game
warden, told me these things. He told me that somebody
was always checking up on Tony: on his life preservers or
his fire extinguishers or his mattresses or his septic tank
or something like that. And whenever Tony looked into
any of these complaints, he usually discovered that they
originated with Howard Willson. Once, he went to ask
Mr. Willson (and Tony told me this himself) if there
wasn't some peaceful way to settle this dispute, or at least
to lay down some rules for fighting fair. But Howard
Willson refused to see Tony; when he saw Tony pull up
in front of the lodge, he went down to the marina and
took one of the launches out to the middle of the lake,
and there he sat, watching the lodge with a pair of binoculars, waiting for Tony to drive away.

In other words, there wasn't much sense in Howard
Willson's attitude toward Tony; consequently, you
wouldn't expect to find much more sense in the attitude
of Don and Dale Willson toward anything or anyone con-
nected with Tony. Actually, Tony seemed like a kind of
family blind spot for the Willsons: just his existing was
enough to throw their metabolism off. However, this
particular story isn't directly about Tony Sauer. It is
about Jesse Christian and Don and Dale . . . and a lot of
the rest of us. The rest of us are involved because—well,
it's a very crooked path: Howard Willson hated Tony
Sauer, so naturally he did not have to look hard to find
a reason to hate Tony's new friend, Jesse. It seems that

9

when Mr. Willson was in the army a gang of Negroes broke open his footlocker and stole over five hundred dollars; Mr. Willson had told this story to his sons often enough that they must have come to believe this was the way Negroes were, *all* Negroes. Therefore, Don and Dale (maybe because they had never known any Negroes personally and were not absolutely positive that all Negroes were thieves, or worse) constantly told us stories about the wild parties and the strange ceremonies *they* were having in Jesse's barn. Don and Dale never said who *they* were—maybe *they* were Indians (there was a Sioux reservation less than fifty miles away), or more Negroes, or even Africans. But once Dale described a bonfire between Jesse's house and his barn; Dale had watched it with his father's binoculars, and there were dark-skinned, nearly naked savages dancing around and around, and sitting on what looked like a throne was a man holding something that looked like a shrunken head.

It was so completely preposterous that naturally we all wanted to believe it. Then too, Don and Dale were by far the finest athletes in Nortonville High School, and none of the rest of us felt entirely competent to correct or ignore the words of someone who could throw a football fifty yards in the air, hit a baseball four hundred feet, and dribble a basketball behind his back. Since most of these marvelous stories about Jesse Christian and his coterie were told in the locker room while Dale's and Don's prowess was still fresh in our minds, we were even less prone to contradict them—it would have been somewhat like stopping a preacher in the middle of his sermon and telling him he didn't know what he was talking about. Maybe he *didn't* know, but he was in his element, and Don and Dale were in their element in the locker room.

And the rest of us were the congregation, the sheep.

Anyway, that's how it all began. There was something dark and horrible and outrageous happening in our midst (the truth is that Jesse Christian was harboring two Indian boys who had escaped from the state reformatory; how and why they came to Jesse is another story). Right now it is important only that you see Don and Dale feeding us visions that were not exactly of sugar plums: visions of obscene dances and lewd embraces. And we bit into those visions, we chewed on them, and they were deliciously sweet. But they were not filling.

This put Don and Dale in a bind. They knew they couldn't go on building us up indefinitely; sooner or later they had to show us something. But once they showed us, we would know as much as they did, and we wouldn't need them anymore to hand out dreams—I suppose what I mean is that each one of us could be his own witch doctor. I would be surprised if any of this went through anybody's mind then (we weren't that self-conscious), but evidently Don and Dale intuitively knew certain things about power.

Or else they were simply liars. Because they told about seven or eight of us to meet at the Point one Saturday night—it was October, with perfect Indian summer weather, the kind that lingers from one week into the next, almost fooling you into thinking there won't be any winter this year. We got together by the marina, and when Dale pointed we could just barely make out Jesse's place.

"Now we'll show you for sure what goes on around there," Don said.

"We'll take the pickup down the lake road and turn down that path that leads to the water, just before his driveway," Dale said.

11

"We don't want anybody to see the pickup from the road," Don added.

"And then you follow us," Dale ordered.

"And do what we say," Don said.

It was like getting ready for a big game: we were anxious and nervous and a little bit frightened, and we all talked at once . . . that is, until we turned onto the lake road and headed south. Dale was driving; Don was sitting with him in the cab, and the rest of us were crowded in the back. Don looked back at us through the broken-out rear window of the cab, and he said, "Now listen to me! I don't know what it is we're going to find or what it is we're going to see. But I just want you guys to realize that we ain't taking you along just for the fun of it. Me and Dale think there's something funny that's going on at this guy's place." Neither Don nor Dale would ever say his name, and this made whatever it was we were going to do or were going to be asked to do easier: it made it impersonal. "I mean, we don't think this guy belongs in our town, and we think it's time somebody did something about it." Then somebody remembered the shrunken head and asked about it. "Well, I'm not saying for sure," Don said, "but all the things we've seen make us think he ought to be taught a good lesson."

The same voice, I think it was Stanley Lester, asked, "You mean we ain't just going out to look around?"

"I ain't saying," Don hissed through the window. "But I just want to find out right now if any of you guys figure you're not real Americans—if you figure you got something better to do than protect the American way of life."

None of us answered. I think it made us all embarrassed for Don, to hear him talking about a crusade when we were preparing for some outdoor window-peeping. And

12

then the uneasiness hit us: what Don said might have *sounded* silly, we might even have laughed at him if he had said it in the locker room, but now we were riding in the back of the Willson truck, Dale was driving, Don was giving orders, and it was like going out to make war.

We left the truck and followed Dale and Don through the fields to the fence that surrounded Jesse Christian's house and barn. Unlike most barns, his had grass growing right up next to it, as though it were living quarters and not just a place for animals. There were no lights either in the house or in the barn, although it was hardly past ten o'clock.

"I guess we ain't going to see anything tonight," said Bobby Miller. And he began to back away.

"Oh, you're going to see something all right, Bobby," said Dale. He took Bobby by the arm and led him back to the truck.

"The rest of you stay here," Don said, "and keep quiet." Don crawled under the barbed-wire fence and peered into one of the barn windows. The sky was clear, but there was only a half-moon, so it was really impossible to say for sure what it was that Don was pointing at when he beckoned for us to come to the window: it was a figure in the straw—it could have been a sheep or a man; it didn't stir. "An animal would have heard us," Don whispered. We looked again, crowding around the window, scraping against the barn, but still there was no stirring, no sound . . . until we heard liquid being splashed against wood. It was Dale with a can of gasoline; he was soaking the east side of the barn, and Bobby was watching. As we turned our attention to them, Bobby grabbed the can and said, "Let me do it, too."

"There's somebody in there," a voice called to Bobby.

13

"I thought there was just him out here," said another voice.

"He's got company all right," said another.

"What did we tell you?" Dale said quietly.

"Who's got matches?" Bobby asked.

"Who wants them?" said Don.

There was a chorus of yelps, and I looked at Stanley Lester, who at the time was my best friend, and he looked at me: we didn't say anything, but I can remember wondering if I looked as frightened as he did. We were in the outer ring around Don, who was holding up the matches while the others reached out for them. We didn't say anything; we simply turned and ran. But we weren't more than twenty-five yards away before we heard a sucking *whoosh* sound and then saw our giant shadows cast by the sudden flame which leapt from Jesse Christian's burning barn.

We never looked back. I imagine the others ran, too, but I never saw them, I never even saw Stanley. I ran across the open field and through a small grove of apple trees at the edge of the field. I never thought to stop there, but went under the fence and then up to the side of the lake road just as a car came down, headed south. It caught me in its headlights, and I stood staring like a spooked deer. The car slipped by me; I watched it go past and then followed it south. I ran all the way home. My parents asked where I'd been. Playing basketball, I said.

Sunday afternoon Stanley Lester and I met downtown; neither of us had heard anything. Apparently Jesse had let the barn burn down without turning in a fire alarm. I mentioned the car; the occupants must have seen me, I said. Stanley said that he had stayed in the grove for several minutes before going home through the fields. The others went with the Willson twins, first north on the lake road and then east to Highway 75 and into Nortonville on that road.

We were standing in front of the Spot 'O' Cream, and Bremer Geare drove past and smiled at us. Bremer was the local chief of police, which meant only that he had under him two men who worked nights and weekends. Bremer was chief mostly because he wanted the job and not many others did. Also, he was not a drinker, and he had once served in the military police in the army. This should have made him a fairly good policeman, except that Bremer never believed that a man was innocent until proven guilty. "I wouldn't be after 'em," Bremer used to say, "unless they'd done something wrong."

"He a friend of yours?" Stanley asked me.

"No, no more than yours," I replied.

And then I felt a mild explosion in my stomach, and my knees began to tremble. *His* car! But, I thought to myself, he would have stopped, he would have done something.

Bremer had parked on a side street. He walked toward us with a big smile on his face. He had marvelously white teeth and a jutting lower jaw. He was fat, but no one called him fat, because "huge" was obviously a more appropriate word: heavy and huge, formidable. He was smiling, his jaw stuck out—and, a few paces away, he winked at me. My mind barely registered the wink before he was standing next to me, leaning over: he's going to grab me! I thought.

"I see you was in on the baptism last night," he said softly.

"The what?"

"That's hot work," he said. "'Course it's one way to

15

make that fellah welcome in the community—really bring him in, uh?"

I tried to smile back at him, but I couldn't work my mouth, or rather my mouth wouldn't work the way I wanted it to.

"Good thing the wind was down," he continued, "or that baptizing might have got out of control." He thought this was very funny; his head lifted up and back, his mouth yawned open, and he bit several times soundlessly into the air. At last he winked. And, speechless still and not knowing what else to do, I winked a broad collaborator's wink. He squeezed my shoulder with his large hand and walked on.

"He knows," Stanley whispered.

I don't remember how I answered him, but I do remember feeling sick, nauseated. I should have felt release, since I knew now who had been in the car and had seen me, and, better yet, I knew I was safe. I think I may have said something about having to go home. As I was walking away Stanley said, "I never did believe that business about a shrunken head."

"Then why did you go along in the first place?" I answered him.

"Did you believe it?"

"If you knew it wasn't so, why didn't you say so?" For some reason my fear was turning into anger.

"I don't think you believed it, either."

"How should I know?" I responded. "They *said*. . . ."

"You don't believe everything they say, do you?"

"I'm not that stupid," I said, and left him.

"You're no better than the rest of us," he called after me.

I went home, but my parents were out for the afternoon,

so I took my bicycle and started up the lake road. It was not until I saw the black skeleton of Jesse's barn that I realized why I had come to this place: to learn if it was really true, if I really had been involved. I never actually saw the fire, except from the road, a safe distance away. And I never touched either the gasoline can or the matches. I never really believed. . . .

Tony Sauer was crossing the field between his place and Jesse's while I was leaning on my bicycle, staring into the space that had once held a red barn. He called to me: "They just let it burn down!" in a tone of outrage that carried clearly across the field to where I was.

"Who did?" I shouted back.

But instead of answering he walked toward me and came beside me. As I said before, Tony taught me everything I know about fishing. You don't necessarily get to know a man well when you go fishing with him; mostly you just sit together and stare over the water and feel one another's presence. Of course, the important thing is that you can *talk* to just about anybody (even if you don't especially like them or have anything in common, you can talk about the weather or baseball or new cars or grass seed), but to sit in silence with another person without feeling the need to talk, to justify your existence together —it may not make the two of you good friends or close friends, but in a funny way it does give you a good sense of being human with another human.

I looked at Tony and, for the first time, I think, noticed how genuinely ugly he was: short, fat, with a lumpy face that some baker might have molded out of dough and then overcooked.

"There ain't nobody knows who did it," he said. "Do you know?"

17

I shook my head No.

"Jesse said they was kids your age. A bunch of kids."

"I just heard about it," I lied. "Downtown."

"Is that the truth?" he asked me.

"Hell, yes," I said.

"You don't have to swear about it," he said.

"You're a fine one to talk," I said. I meant for the words to come out lightly, jokingly. But they sounded harsh to my ear, grating.

"Only when it's appropriate," he answered.

It was an unlikely word for him to use: "appropriate." Somehow it made him sound like a teacher. "I've got to get back home," I said. I turned my bike around, got on and rode toward town. Tony stood there and watched; I'm certain he did, although I didn't turn around to look.

On my way back I was met by one car, a navy blue Lincoln: Howard Willson's car. He was driving. Beside him sat Bremer Geare. Bremer was smiling; Mr. Willson waved at me and smiled, too. And then the car was past and I was engulfed in a swirl of dust left from summer.

After that, nothing really happened. I went home, I ate, I watched television until ten o'clock, I went to bed—and in bed I cried for the first time in years. And I tried to pray. I thought of God's eye upon me, and saw Bremer's wink, and then the Lincoln and Howard Willson's open-handed wave. I felt lost, and when I finally slept I thrashed through bad dreams having to do with being chased and finding no place to hide. In one of the dreams I tried to hide in a church, but there was a service in progress. Bremer was preaching. I don't remember what he was saying, only that he interrupted his sermon several times to laugh. It seemed that he was laughing at me, and as he laughed a fine spray of spittle struck my face.

18

Monday at the supper table my father mentioned the barn burning. He was the postmaster, so he usually got the latest news in town—I don't mean from reading postcards, but from people coming and staying a few minutes to pass the time of day; in a small town just about the whole population drops into the post office at least once a day. I asked him who had burned the barn, and he said that quite a few suspected Tony Sauer. "They think," he said, "that Tony probably got drunk and had a fight with this fellow and got mad and burned down his barn."

"But they're friends!" I blurted out.

"Well, now," my father said, "whiskey does funny things to people."

"But couldn't it have been somebody else?" I was on the verge of confessing until I recalled that I had touched neither the gas can nor the matches: "Like . . . somebody else?"

"Such as?" my father asked.

But I veered away. "Are they going to help him rebuild his barn?" It was customary, if a farmer lost a barn or house to fire or lightning or wind, for his friends and neighbors and even the people in town to get together and contribute money and labor to put the building up again. Of course, if the farmer was insured they might not give any money, but they always gave a day or half a day of labor, because whether it was a house or a barn the farmer needed it to live in or to keep his cattle or his feed in, and he couldn't wait for a couple of carpenters to build it at their own pace.

"I didn't know he used it," my father said.

"I think he had some stock in it," I said. "At least he got it all fixed up after he moved there. He must have used it for something."

"I wouldn't know," my father said.

"Nobody mentioned anything about helping him with it?" I asked.

"Nobody said anything to me," he said, "except that it burned down. But if you're so interested, why don't you go out and help him?"

Needless to say, I kept far from Jesse's place until long after the new barn was up. Tony Sauer helped Jesse with the building, and this merely confirmed what most people thought: Tony had done it while drunk. There were some of us who knew better, but we kept quiet about it.

Jesse

Take a number yes sir stand in line wait for bread number thirteen what does that mean thirteen no luck no I'm not a superstitious man "Well, I waited, Tony," he said. "I never believed you."

"I told you," Tony said.

"I know what you told me. But I didn't believe you."

"Maybe you were born unlucky. Did you ever consider that?"

"I was born black" *born under a black star carry the night with me dark black it all stands for evil I bear evil heap it on* "It's the same thing."

Tony took the thermos and poured the rest of the coffee into the two cups. He leaned against a stack of shingles and said: "I don't know why you don't leave well enough alone."

"Are you still talking about the bread?"

"No. The barn. They burned it down; it'd be cheaper to seed it over with grass. They wouldn't come out here again just to burn a patch of grass."

"Maybe I'm going to buy some cattle."

"That's your business."

"Must be lots of people's business." He drank the coffee, then slipped the hammer into the loop on his overalls and climbed the ladder up to the unfinished roof. "Like Ben Carlson," he called down. "He seemed to take it real personal."

"Maybe he's superstitious," Tony said. "He don't like to call out number thirteen. You should have had twelve. Or fourteen."

Tony handed him a pack of shingles, and joined him on the roof. The sun was high and there was no shade, but a light breeze off the lake dried their sweat *He called number ten good busy bakery so good bread Carlson the baker fat pasty pastry-pasty all in white bread-priest dealing out the sacrament* Number eleven *he sees me* Hold up your numbers, please. Hold up your numbers so I can see *yes of course forgive me father for I have not tasted your bread and I am hungry* Number twelve *good he knows I am next poor man barn burned down but no sorries here black man eats white bread racial mixing Lord why did I ever look talking to bread-buying lady filling a box with loaves too much for one family* Thank you, Carlson said. Thank you very much, Mrs. Willson *did I ever come here wandering well stay where you belong not here Lord I would like to knead that face lump knead knee knee-up hear his squeal piglike oinkoinkoink pig-priest calls number fourteen* Wait. Excuse me, he said *excuse forgive forgive hell I damn near have tears in my eyes rolling down fighting them tell me to love Lord tell me to love and I will spit in your face* Who's next? Number fourteen *don't tell me this is the worst that ever happened Carlson looks at me skips over me asks me don't tell me this is the worst I ask it too answer it too half a smile for him let him know I know no this is not the worst the worst is yet to come keep thinking that believe it the worst Carlson is nothing you could roll on my black head God knows yes God knows simple faith of the disinherited* I believe you skipped a number, he said. Carlson, busy wrapping a dozen cinnamon rolls, said, You'll have to take a number; no one is served without a number. Looking up, he called, Fifteen. Fifteen next, please.

Tony said it quietly, slowly, as though he had been meditating on it for a long time: "Don't you know this is a friendly community? It says so right on that sign just outside of town."

"Maybe not everybody's got around to reading it yet." Jesse buried another nail through shingle and timber with a short, violent stroke.

God knows you don't Tony blessed Tony you'd build for me Tony get blisters and sweat for me but not know not die for me I have to do that dive into Carlson's dough and drown sink into that lardbelly and die hear dying that rumbling laugh Number sixteen next *wait you forgot you forgot no not forgot but remembered I am Africa fatherless child serpent and sin not fit for white bread Adam madam I'm Adam lock up your daughters the dungman all waste and woolly is loose but not devouring God knows not devouring bearing I will feel no self-pity feel no self-pity no self-pity God knows I want too a shoulder to cry on God's got no shoulders God knows I bear up the worst's yet to come*

Outside, she was wrestling the box into the back seat of her car. He stood behind her and asked, Do you need some help?

It sure looks that way, she said.

So he opened the front door and pulled while she pushed, hair in her eyes. The smile trembled briefly on her lips, dropped. I could have handled it, she said.

What did you say to that man? Jesse asked her.

23

Nothing, she said. I asked him how much the bread was.

I thought you might have been talking about me. Or perhaps I was being overly sensitive.

Not necessarily. In fact, you may not be sensitive enough. She used the back door like a kind of shield between Jesse and herself. You see, we don't exactly approve of the things that go on at your place.

You mean the fire? I don't exactly approve, either.

With the wind in the wrong direction, there could have been a lot of damage. That would make a lot of people very angry.

I've had people angry with me before, he said.

Well, we don't like the idea of your bringing in those Indians to. . . . She stopped. Jesse looked around to see if anyone was approaching. No one was; there were only the two of them, separated by the car door and the unfinished sentence: no more to say.

Your sons, he began. But she turned, in turning closed the door, and walked away from him.

"We're going to have too many shingles," Tony said. They were in the shade of the barn now, eating sandwiches that Tony's wife had fixed, cold fish.

"Do you really know who did it?" Jesse asked him.

"Willson boys," Tony said.

"Did you see them?"

"I heard the truck drive away. I know the sound of that truck."

"I met Mrs. Willson on the street the other day. She said she didn't like Indians."

"That's not all she doesn't like. I suspect that we're both on her list, too."

"But how do we know it wasn't the Indians?"

"I heard the truck. I went outside and I saw the flames and I heard Willson's truck drive down the lake road."

"But maybe she doesn't know that," Jesse said.

"I told you, you ought to keep those damn kids out of here," Tony said.

"Which kids?"

"The Indian kids. What they can give you is trouble, and that's about all."

Jesse laughed. "Maybe I should tell the grass to stop growing, too."

"It's not the same thing," Tony said. "I mean, you could try locking your doors for a change, and you could padlock the barn here."

Jesse shook his head No.

"Well," Tony said, "if you like trouble, that's your business, only I want you to know that I don't plan to come over here every week to rebuild your barn."

"They were on their way to Minneapolis," Jesse said. "Three of them. One had a brother who'd been through before."

"Just because you made a mistake once, you don't have to keep making it."

"You don't know what you're talking about," Jesse said. He put a handful of nails into his pocket and climbed the ladder *we ain't got no room in this here inn*

"Hell, no," Tony said. "But I've never had any of my buildings burned down. Of course that might change too, now that I'm helping you on this." He followed Jesse up the ladder.

Homer where did that come from Homer Goodthunder yes I remember him and you're his brother Hector three children Greeks bearing tales adept yes most adept at lying going to school we're going to go to school in Minneapolis

25

*our sister is married and we're going to stay with her
among themselves they spoke their own tongue wait don't
you understand I'm one of you speak with me speak O
Hector brother of Homer speak of the sea and the long
march upcountry across the straits Bering Strait and now
what you've lost your bearings it's a long way back and
you're not wanted do you remember that in your blood
the long trip across ice snow and winter without relent on
something less than even moccasins and I know it too only
my story's in the hold of a ship as dark as the ace of spades
the death card spades for digging and dying and being
black for the world speak my tongue I see you do called
Pain*

"Feel that wind," Tony said. "The Northerns'll be
biting in those rocks about a hundred yards off the point
just before the sun goes down."

"Is that an invitation?" Jesse asked *You'll have to stay
in the barn but the straw is clean and I've got some extra
blankets now read it Brother of Homer Thalassa thalassa
the sea first smell of home for the Greeks* You wonder why
I want to teach you Greek, Jesse? Yessir. So that I will not
forget it myself. Did you think I had a nobler motive? I
didn't know. No, of course not, what would you know
about noble motives? Hulking man, medicine man,
pickled snakes, syphilitic brains, fetuses curled in dumb
wonderment, all in a row, like a woman's canning, on top
of the cabinet he called his tool chest, he sat in the swivel
chair holding aloft Xenophon's *Anabasis* like a sacrament.
He, whom no woman in the county could trust, and none
now did, but the Negroes—only because he was cheap: a
baby for a sack of potatoes, a broken arm set for fifty
cents, sometimes a nickel, if he'd been drinking, an appendix taken out for a dollar (in his office: a whiff of

chloroform, a fogged image of pickled death), no guarantees and not much hygiene, and never knowing when the innoculation, vaccination for Rocky Mountain Spotted Fever, suddenly, gratuitously, earnestly prescribed might drowsily draw doctor and patient into sodden fornication: he, bug-eyed, thick-lensed glasses . . . (All I could see was them damn glasses like two spotlights shining into me and I wanted so damn bad to smash 'em, only I couldn't make my hands work, couldn't even feel my hands: O Lord, I don't know what was in that damn needle, but I think he was the one with the fever.)

Did you trim the hedges like I told you? he asked Jesse. Yessir. And now you're ready for the lesson? Yessir. Maybe you'd rather read the Bible; would you? You're the boss. That's in Greek too; did you know that? Yessir, now you told me. Iesus Xristos Theos Uios Soter: IXTHUS: the fish: do you know what that means? No sir. It means that you're a damned fish. Yessir. You don't need to come up for air. Now say, Thalassa. Thalassa. Do you know what it means? No sir. The sea. It means, the sea. That's your element; you sink in it and you don't drown. Now, next question: what's my element? Dry land? Dry land. Dry land is dust, man is dust, and therefore man is dry land. Yessir *ninety and nine safely in the fold* "I can't work tomorrow," Tony said. "I got to take some people fishing. From Iowa."

"That's work too, isn't it?"

"All I do is tell 'em where to drop anchor and what bait to use. And then I try hard not to catch more than they do."

"I guess I can manage the rest of it myself."

"I can come the day after if you still got work to do."

"Do you like fish?" Jesse asked.

"To eat?"

"No, just as fish. Like you like dogs. Or cats."

"It's not the same."

"Didn't you ever feel sorry," Jesse asked, "when you pull one in and you see him gasping, fighting to get back into the water, with those eyes staring at you?"

"I always give 'em a fair chance."

"But you don't have anything to lose."

"The way I look at it, you can't worry about everything. If nobody fished, then the lake'd get overstocked, and there wouldn't be enough oxygen to go around, so they'd die that way. Or else the bigger fish'd eat the smaller ones. Like me and Willson. He's been fishing for me, and he doesn't feel sorry. And I don't expect him to. I just keep busy trying to stay alive."

"You're right in the middle then, aren't you?"

"I guess you could say that."

"Let's finish the rows we're on," Jesse said, "and then we'll go out on the lake" *fifty cents he paid for trimming the hedges cutting the grass weeding Nunley's office was in back walk up the front steps turn left follow the veranda to the left until it ended with the door and the little tin sign Doctor's Office* I'm glad you knocked; when you're twelve you should always knock before you open a closed door; you never know what you'll uncover; a twelve-year-old boy cannot be too careful of his moral fibre. Have you ever seen your moral fibre, boy? No sir. Do you want me to show it to you? Uh. No sir. That's good. Never trust an old man. Isn't that right? Whatever you say, sir. Yessir. Yessir. All right. And now you want to get paid? I just came to tell you I'm all finished. And now it's time for a little Greek, right? Yessir. Then give me some Greek, boy. Thalassa. That's good, very good. He reached into his

28

pocket and took out a dollar bill. There, he said, handing it to Jesse. Do you know what the extra four bits is for? No sir. Is it for the Greek? If you say so. It's for the baptism. You were baptized last Sunday, weren't you? Yessir. Just like a fish, boy. Yessir. You went down the third time and you could tell it was your element, you didn't have to come up for air. Oh, yessir. I'm a Baptist too. Did you know that? No sir. An unbaptized Baptist. That ought to send me to hell for sure, don't you think? No sir. Then what's the point of going through with it?

Eight of them. It was hot and he was the eighth, the creek was roiled, muddy, and inside the white gown he was drenched in sweat. Reverend Holly stood in water up to his chest. During the first baptism he was in only up to his waist; but with each successive one he inched, or was inched, farther along. His voice grew weaker. Between each baptism the congregation on the bank sang a hymn, and the newly baptized sprang out of the water to be received, enfolded by a tearfully joyous mother, then aunts and cousins too *the words I can't hear them any more dimmer and dimmer we are floating away and the water is still and he is God in the mud of the beginning is was will be baptizing just like this forever and ever and at last the heat rising in breathless prehistoric waves from that pool of our birthing his benedictioning hands beckoned me at last into the water the last last of the lost Mother nudged me I left the shore surprised the water was as cold as it was I walked toward him and the water rose and Reverend Holly stood with his arms raised monster of the deep waiting to snare me kidnap me into his terrible hiding place under the waves looked into me past me and saw nothing but my soul the bottom of the creek was mud*

felt good soft I sank into it went down with his hand on
my head fought up for air sobbed went down again longer
this time I thought he's forgot forgot and then up and
down not hearing any words not seeing faces only feeling
that hand vise driving me down feeling that hand tighten
stiffen relax that body slip down lightly firmly onto my
shoulder throwing me off balance drowning me I thought
drowning me murdering

Do you still knock? the doctor asked. Everytime? Yessir,
the boy said. How old are you now? Seventeen. That
means it's six years we've been together, boy. Yessir, six
years in May. We ought to drink to that, boy. What do
you think? I'm not old enough.

Unchanged, he sat like a weary Buddha in the swivel
chair. There was a bottle on his desk—no, technically, a
fruit jar—and a glass in his hand. You've got character, boy,
he said. I am going to put you into my will. Said with no
apparent premeditation: one remark lapping upon the
preceding one, pointlessly. He reached into his desk and
took out a brown folder, which he showed to the boy,
pointing to the words penciled across the folder, reading
them in a halting, mocking tone: Last Will and Testa-
ment. He opened the folder, took out a single sheet, a
clean, white sheet, except for several lines typed at the top.
This here's going to be a codicil. Do you know what the
hell a codicil is? No sir. Well, you just listen, and I'll give
you an example. He spoke the words slowly as he wrote
them down: I hereby bequeath to Jesse Christian twenty
per cent of my estate, following liquidation of all real
assets and payment of all legal fees, taxes, et cetera. The
boy sat expressionless. The doctor rose and opened the
door to the right of his desk. Mary Jane, he called, and the
boy could see a figure move on what appeared to be a table

in the middle of the newly opened room. Move your ass out here.

She held a sheet around her body; she moved slowly, looked straight ahead, glassy-eyed. She's had surgery, the doctor explained. Show him where. Mary Jane smiled, said nothing, stood still in the doorway. Show him, he ordered. Ear, she said. Infection, said the doctor. Had to puncture the ear drum, let the pus run out. How do you feel now? Mary Jane nodded her head, slowly. Do you feel good enough to sign your name here? He held out the will and a pen, and she crossed to take them. As she reached, he grabbed the sheet from her, and she stood naked between the man and the boy. No one spoke: the boy stared, Mary Jane continued to smile vaguely, the man laid the paper on his desk, gave her the pen, and drew a line with his finger where she should sign. Under her signature he printed: WITNESS, then dated the codicil and filed it in the folder and put the folder into the desk again. She feels no pain, he said. Isn't that wonderful? She looked around for her sheet, but he kicked it under his desk. You always knocked, he said to the boy. There ought to be some sort of reward for that, don't you think? The boy said nothing. The doctor reached for his glass, emptied it, and filled it again.

You don't have to worry, he said. She's twenty-one. By suppertime she'll be home, she'll never know the difference. Neither Mary Jane nor the boy spoke; it seemed as though Mary Jane was trying to remember something. She stopped smiling and folded her arms over her breasts. It's old Miz Holly's granddaughter, he said. Down here for a visit. Don't you want to make her feel welcome?

What did you do to her? the boy asked.

The doctor sat down behind his desk, drank again,

sighed. She came in, she was full of pain; I made her well. She likes it. Suddenly he stood up and leaned over the desk, pointing his finger at the boy: She likes it; I healed her. So don't you be so damn superior. Don't you think that just because you came around here year after year and always knocked on the damn door that you're better than anyone else: you stink, just like the rest of 'em. And I'm better than the whole lot of you. I did her a favor. Do you hear that? I did her a favor!

Now their eyes met, the boy's and the girl's, as he turned away from the doctor. And she dropped to her knees and searched for the sheet. Do you see what you're doing? the doctor shouted. You're getting her stirred up. One hand raised the glass to his mouth, the other took the folder from the desk; one foot kicked the sheet away from Mary Jane, kicked it into the room where she had been. On hands and knees she crawled after the sheet, until he intercepted her and pulled her to her feet. I know what your trouble is, he said to the boy, while he held her arm. You're embarrassed, aren't you? He said it gently, in the same tone in which he used to pronounce *thalassa*: soothing sibilants. Releasing her arm, he watched her sink to the floor again, and he stood over her and unbuckled his belt, unzipped his pants, let them fall around his ankles, unbuttoned his shirt and slipped it off, pulled down his shorts: naked too, though his ankles were cuffed. There now, he smiled. Isn't that better? Now there's nothing to be shy about. Mary Jane lay still on the floor, asleep. I'm talking about power, boy, the doctor said. Now just look at it, he said, looking down at himself, that wasted, wrinkled, motionless member. . . . You could be a better man than I am, boy, if you just wanted.

The boy turned away. You knocked, the doctor said.

You wanted to come in, so don't be so damn superior. Her grandfather baptized me, the boy said *in the water his weight dead I didn't know I had to get up fight he held me down held me into the mud and I struggled they said I walked out of the water with him still on my back carried him so that it looked like he was floating and he was a big man way over two hundred I don't remember it he came down on me and I rose again from the dead they started with artificial respiration and one man started for the doctor but his wife said heart attack it's no use he's in glory the man went instead for the undertaker we picked up everything and began to leave and Miz Holly sang took up moaning the same song that had been sung all day take me to the water take me to the water take me to the water to be baptized none but the righteous none but the righteous none but the righteous shall see God four men carried Reverend Holly bearing him to God and Miz Holly followed holding on to me risen from the dead in my damp angel gown he passed it on to you she said you got the power now she said you gonna be the man now for him she said* He's dead, the doctor said, and there ain't nothing you can do to hurt him. Or him you.

The boy said no more. Go on, now, the doctor said. I'm gonna let you be a man, just like you're one of my own. He waved the folder, lurched forward, fell on his face. Damn you! he said to the boy. What's the matter with you? He tried to get up, but his feet were tangled in his pants and he rolled over on top of Mary Jane, who only moaned. And the boy got up to help the man. Here, the boy said, extending his hand. And the man took his hand, jerked hard, and pulled the boy down, so that he lay across the man's chest, their faces nearly touching. Now what do you think? the man hissed. We're on the same level. Do you

33

want to fight for her? Would that make it better for you, to fight? All right, I give up, I surrender, you're a better man than I am, I'm all dried up, wasted away. You go on in and I'll guard the door for you; I'll be like a slave, how do you like that, I'll be a harmless slave. Panting whiskey-breathing into the boy's face, he bared his teeth in a broad grin and rolled his eyes: Yassuh, yassuh, boss; you bet, boss; you're the boss all right, yassuh, yassuh. But the boy rolled away, stood up, backed against the desk. No, he said. I'm not going to. And he watched, fascinated, as the man, more agile than he expected, got to his knees, then to his feet. Like a boy in a sack race he hopped to the desk, pushed Jesse aside, and searched under the papers until he found a book of matches. All right, he said. How many chances do you think I'm going to give you?

Gnosis was another word thalassa and gnosis the Greeks had a word for it everything and if you weren't so damn slow maybe you'd have the words too yessir yessir yessir is that all you can say no wonder you don't know Greek I'm giving you a blessed gift and you don't even know what it's all about yessir it's so you won't forget it you told me gnosis means knowledge eros is love and here's a funny one eremos is both desert and loneliness a lonely desert a dry place a dry self ho thalassa the Greek warriors cried and I boy sit in this dry room trying to give you hope elpis in Greek pistis is faith elpis pistis eros hope faith love from a dry man looking for thalassa well you've already found it thalassa ho thalassa is that what he said old Holly is that what he said when he ducked you down no sir what did he say then I don't remember he never knew the doctor how he died we kept it quiet like we always kept our private life quiet they knew enough the way it was he died we mourned let them guess the rest he glided over thalassa

on the barque of my back into glory what is Greek for
glory it doesn't matter we never got that far it was over
and over ho thalassa learn Greek boy and the world's your
oyster a man with a command of languages has got the
lever to tip over the world yessir Well, how many chances?
he shouted. I don't know, the boy said.

I'm set to give you white man's cash. He waved the
folder under the boy's nose. You can buy your people out
of slavery, he said. They ain't in slavery, the boy said. Like
hell, the man said. They are in slavery, and here's the key
to unlock the door. Now move off and mount up. The boy
hung on to the desk, bracing himself. Go on, get busy, the
man said. Or else I burn the will. Take your choice. The
boy spoke no answer, only shook his head No. No? the
man asked, lowering, softening his voice; then, surprised,
Is that right? I find that hard to believe. Calmly he lighted
a match and set fire to the folder. Isn't that something, he
said. Your future's going up in smoke. How do you feel?
The boy whispered hoarsely, I'm all right. Yes, I'm sure
you are, the man said, his voice rising again. You have
thrown away the world, you have sold out your people,
you have wasted your greatest opportunity, and inspired
by ignorance you claim to be all right. You, boy, have a
naked, cheap, tawdry mind that's fit for no more than
hatching flies and sucking eggs.

Hell, said the boy, finding his voice again.

To hell with you, boy, the man said. His eyes narrowed,
the flames curled around his wrist and fingers, and he
dropped the burning folder to the floor, watched it burn,
lick into the old wood and spread out aimlessly. To hell
with you, he said, staring into the fire. And then the boy
left the desk and went to stamp out the fire. And after that
the boy walked to the door.

35

You come back next week, d'ya hear? he shouted. You're still working for me, you better not forget it. I'm gonna look for you, and there'll be hell to pay in this town if I don't see you here next week out in that damn yard.

I'll be here, the boy said, letting himself out.

And don't forget to knock, can you remember that?

I'll remember, the boy said to himself as he walked down the veranda.

You knock, you always knock, he cried, and he reached down, groped for his shorts and pants. The girl, Mary Jane, stirred briefly, slept on *thirteen thirteen years now more or less no exactly that's funny there have been worse things might as well laugh* "Look here, Tony," he said. "Why do people hate peace so much?"

"They don't," Tony said. "Not individually."

"That's true, I guess. We use other people like talismans, that's the trouble."

"I don't know what you're talking about," Tony said.

"I mean, we ought to be more reckless," he said.

"Hell, yes," Tony said. "Like encouraging kids to drive eighty, ninety up the lake road; like walking off the roof of this barn; that makes a lot of sense."

"You don't know what I'm talking about."

"Maybe it's the heat," Tony said. "It's affecting both of us."

"Listen," Jesse said, stopping with the last shingle of the row in his hands. "Listen, if we were out in the middle of the lake and I told you to get out of the boat and walk on the water, I mean, if I told you it was going to be all right, if I told you that I love you too much to let anything bad happen to you, would you try it?"

"Hell no," Tony said. "I'll shingle the barn for you, but I'm not that crazy."

36

"That's what I mean," he said. They finished the shingling and climbed down to the ground. After the tools were put away, Jesse got the tackle and bait together, Tony got the boat ready, and then Jesse rowed. Tony guided them along the shore until they reached the place, half a mile up the lake from Jesse's and about forty yards offshore, where Tony said, "Drop it," and Jesse let down the concrete weight that was their anchor.

"You're sure the Indian boys didn't start it?" Jesse asked.

"I already told you what I heard, that truck, Willson's truck, I'll swear to it. I saw the fire, and next I heard the truck start up. You figure it out."

"So what do I say when then they come again?"

"Who? Willson's kids?"

"The Indians," Jesse said. "Should I tell them there's no room in the inn?"

"Why not, unless one of 'em's pregnant?"

"The squaws stay home, the braves go out," Jesse said. "That's a beautiful name, isn't it? Brave. It's better than mister, by a long way. It tells you something about yourself."

"Except they got no way to earn it any more. No buffalo to shoot, no battles to fight."

"Except with themselves."

"And then who's to tell them if they've won or not?"

"One of the boys had a war bundle with him," Jesse said. "Did you ever see a war bundle?"

"That's just what they need, all right, is something to start a war with," Tony said. "Well, I suppose they got nothing to lose."

"Hector had it, Hector Goodthunder. It was a little package covered with canvas and tied with leather thongs. Actually, he wasn't supposed to have it. He said there was only supposed to be one in the Turtle Clan, but somehow it fell into the hands of a fellow named Fred Blowsnake, and one night in a bar in North Dakota Fred traded it to a truck driver for a drink. Nobody ever said much about it; nobody really accused Fred Blowsnake, ever lost his temper or threatened poor Fred—so Hector told me—but just the same there were a number of people in the clan who felt they'd been betrayed. Well, it was just one more thing lost; one more step, I suppose, in the process of becoming new Americans.

"The old war bundle had the remains of an eagle and a hawk and a snake. And a weasel skin and a buffalo tail and the paw of a wolf. And I guess there was some war paint, and some powder made by crushing and mixing up an elk's antlers and pipe stone. It all meant something. Hector remembered what was in the bundle, but that's what he didn't remember very well: what it meant. He said it had to do with courage and fast running and good shooting—generalities. Except that Hector didn't need generalities; he needed a real, genuine wolf's paw to hang on to, to show him how to claw his way."

"If he's like most of the kids from that reservation, what he needed was a good kick in the pants and a haircut. And a bath," Tony said.

"He showed me the war bundle he'd put together," Jesse said. "There was a Captain Marvel comic book. And he'd taken a red pencil and colored Captain Marvel's face red. And there was an empty rifle cartridge and an arrowhead that he'd found in a grove near his home. There was a handful of teeth he'd knocked out of the skull of a dead coyote. And a couple of pocket gopher skins. They smelled pretty bad, and he apologized that he didn't know how to cure them. Finally he took the skins out of the package and threw them away. That was before the fire. The other two boys were sleeping in the barn, and we were having coffee in the kitchen. He said he couldn't sleep. . . . Oh yes, I almost forgot: the last item in his bundle, a ball point pen. I don't know what made me ask him if it worked, but I did. So he took the pen and tried to make marks with it on his arm. But nothing showed, and finally he snapped the pen in two and left it on my table when he tied up the bundle. I told him I was sorry, and he shouldn't have broken the pen, because it was a good sign for eloquence and wise talking. But he said, 'It's just junk, it's a lot of junk.' And then he left for the barn.''

"Can't understand it," Tony said, lifting his line and throwing it in again on the other side of the boat.

"Can't understand what?" Jesse asked.

"They're not biting," he said.

"Want to try someplace else?"

"If they're not biting here, they won't be biting any-place else, either."

It got dark early then, almost the middle of October, but the temperature hung in the seventies and eighties, Indian summer, lingering into the third week, as if it might stay through December. At seven the lake was dark, but the water was warm; weary oarlocks scraped against wood, motors started and buzzed like giant insects startled awake and angry. No fish anywhere, all of them deep down where it was cool, curling around the cool rocks. A hand dipped into the water came up green, but at least there were not so many mosquitoes as a month before. And they sat still *found him dead with a gun we sat mother and I black folk rocking on the porch ain't no news no never news old and ever unconsummated dreams who finished high school dropped out joined the army*

*tried college but Jesse he's a preacher just a boy but he
even got into Oklahoma they found him in his office and
he was wearing a dress that's all he had on the boy found
him Louis Wister he worked for the doctor just like you
did cut the grass trimmed the hedge the doctor he wasn't
much good for nothing old and fat sometimes people come
in to see him and he'd sit behind his desk wouldn't say
hello good morning nothing just sit and stare you'd have
to walk out and go someplace else Louis found him well
Louis did you ever expect what you found what did he
say nothing he didn't say nothing did you hear anything
did he leave anything behind had something written on
him right on his chest in lipstick some kind of funny word
began with a T like Talahassee maybe it was THALASSA
Talahassee like maybe that's where he wanted to be buried
I didn't know he knew anybody in Talahassee that's in
Florida that's what it says*

"Let's go back," Tony said. But neither of them moved
*that's what it says he left you twenty thousand there'll be
less with taxes and fees taken out but still enough left over
so you can get into some other racket boy well the way it
happened the way he did what he did Bond smiling I-hate-
you smile you are not my client my office does not need
want desire solicit take in any manner whatsoever hereto-
fore in any way shape or form non habeas corpus nothing
since you are all crap to us the way it happened it is fitting
you get it no self-respecting whiteman would want to
touch it tainted like it is maybe we ought to have it
marked with his lipstick and that word I don't give a damn
personally what it means and do not intend to find out
because I know the rotten condition of his burned-out
mind coming from the kind of practice that sought him
out well it is now too late for you to redeem his soul maybe*

you can find some way to send the money down to hell
with him or maybe you will just raise hell with the money
go to hell with it as far as I am concerned and after no
stand quiet head bowed oh boss you am raising scars with
that terrible sharp tongue but this poor black boy he sure
do deserve every scar on his dirty crap back lash away
mister lawyer and how much finally how much ten thou-
sand that's how much the rest in taxes and fees fees for
Mister Bond all that dirty money he cleaned up because
it went through my pocket and that's all right because all
they want to do is sit and rock sit and rock and you know
what else we do not have to discuss that in polite society
but we know Mister Bond knows he is a fine bourbon-
drinking gentleman and hears much behind his locked
doors from other fine bourbon-drinking gentlemen crap
is what they are it is smeared on they attract it through his
pocket all that money and the swill and crap on it rubbed
off on him and now I am Mister Bond and I have clean
money in my pockets he has the crap crap attracts crap
clean gravitates to clean I am clean I wish you never heard
of the man, his mother said.

But the fact is that I have, Jesse said. And it's not a bad
feeling to have ten thousand dollars.

You'll never preach again, she said.

Why do you say that?

It wouldn't be right, she said. Not with that man's
money in your pocket. Here Jesus throws them bankers
out of the church that time, and you come in with their
money in your pocket. You can't serve two masters.

He was a doctor, he wasn't a banker.

That don't make no difference, she said. You know what
I mean. You ain't got no business preaching to people as
long as you're carrying that money.

Maybe I never intended to keep on being a preacher, he said.

Reverend Claymore says you been doing a fine job, she said.

Reverend Claymore says whatever comes into his mind, he said.

Reverend Claymore says he took you along just to sing in the quartet, she said. And you wasn't with him more'n three months and he had you making one of the sermons.

I asked for money, that's what the sermon was all about; I stood up and I begged, he said. Not for the Lord Jesus Christ, mind you; I begged so I could have ham and eggs for breakfast in the morning; that's why I was good, because I wanted to keep my stomach full, and the better I talked the more money came in and the better I ate. Is that the kind of preaching you want me to do? Is that so much better than taking the money off a crazy doctor who shot himself?

Well, she said, rocking *endlessly rocking thalassa ho thalassa uncontradicting simply being saying one thing then another calm and rough any and everything always ending up I am your mother not what I say but who we are mother and son lapping over and around you wearing and shaping this way and that this is my son after which there can be no contradictions all is an unfolding out of that dearly nurtured seed* You could go to college, you've got the money for it.

So he went two years to a little Baptist college in Texas, dropped out, was called up for the draft but failed his physical: heart murmur, they tested him four times over three months, and he said he'd never had any trouble, but each time the cardiograph registered, the cardiogram recorded, the doctors pointed to a series of jagged lines that indicated malfunction: A broken heart, he told his mother, for which there is no known cure. And then *these hands that hold this pole will someday turn cold deathly cold I can't believe it I know it's so*

Tony took the oars from the bottom of the boat, slipped them into the locks and began to row. "It better not be this way tomorrow," he said, "or I might lose some good customers" *You'll go fast they promised is that a promise really yes really you'll go fast won't know what hit you who knows you might live another thirty forty fifty years and then BANG you won't know what hit you it's a blessing really no I don't believe it no across from me the mirror said it too NO this flesh cannot believe death into the valley of it walking God hold my hand see you do believe I do believe Reverend Claymore I do now look he said we have got to find some people around here to be healed we cannot have them from this same town because we never know about whether their relatives will show up so I want you Jesse to go over to Arco tonight and find yourself the poorest part of town and recruit three four people one for lameness another for stomach trouble and one for headaches you know how to tell 'em symptoms and all that we pay fifteen dollars fifteen dollars for maybe an hour's work is pretty good a damn sight better than shoveling up mister charlie's shit Healings Every Night said the sign healings singing preaching special prayers for the sick* He put the money, cash, into a metal box, locked it, put that into a larger metal box, locked that too, buried it in a grove close to the place where he'd been baptized, and began his wandering. You could go back to school, his mother said. I could drop dead, he said, studying the square root of Chaucer. You ought to be a preacher. That's what Reverend Holly said. That's right, he said, only first I got to find my flock. God, he'll find a flock for you if you tell him you're ready to follow him. What about the money? he asked. Do you want the money? No. You could live like a queen, he said. I'll leave that up to God. If he wants me to be a queen, he'll provide the crown *well I have to bear that too that faith that dirty money thirteen wait you forgot no omitted bear that too bring all those things together America THE BEAUTI-FUL thy rocks and rills thy shining hills from sea to shining sea shining flashlight in the eyes nightstick slapped against soles swift beating GET OUT OF HERE GET OUT OUT DAMNED SPOT HAHAHAHAHA and happened to see sitting in Des Moines a place by a lake for sale dug up the money passed her grave shed no tears she has her crown she's been found remembered that from all that time ago she's got her crown now it's my turn America find me God find my America deliver it to me here in this boat the land drifts by the stationary boat the stick in the water is really bent the illusion is the reality the reality is the rising up from this water living I HAVE A DESTINY GOD A DESTINY BLACKNESS BROKEN HEART AND CROWN* Tony rowed. Far across the lake the tiny loons be-gan their maniac hooting *sink that self in the water money in the soil it is all we can do all is to wait for resurrection not believe it that's not the most important thing not believing just waiting and going on bearing sinking bearing*

"Do you want to hear a story?" he asked Tony.

"If you want to tell it," Tony said. "I hope it isn't about fish."

"No, it's a religious story. Hector told it to me. It's about an old man who goes to visit the sun, and while he's there the two of them get hungry, so they decide to go hunting. Then the sun takes out this magnificent pair of leggings, embroidered with what looks like gold and silver thread, and he pulls them on—the old man has got to shield his eyes for the brightness—and off they go. They come down to this thick brush where they're pretty sure the deer are, only it's too tangled for them to walk into and still have their bows ready for shooting. The old man figures they might as well walk on, since the deer are not going to be so dumb as to leave their safety just to get shot. But the sun tells him that these are very special leggings; all the sun has to do is walk around this brush and the leggings will set it on fire, and the blaze will drive out the deer, force them right into the path of the hunters. Well, this is what happens, the sun walks around the brush, the brush burns, the deer leap out, and the two hunters each shoot a deer. That night, after they've had a good meal, they lay down to sleep. Right away the sun goes sound asleep, but the old man rolls and stirs, and finally he admits to himself that the trouble is envy: he just plain has to have those leggings. So he gets up and he goes over where the sun is sleeping, and the leggings are laying beside him, and the old man takes them and runs. He runs for a couple of miles, until he figures he's far enough away from the house of the sun that he can rest in safety. He sits down, rolls up the leggings for a pillow, and before he knows it, he's sound asleep too.

"It's light when he wakes up, and the sun is standing over him. The old man looks around and he discovers he's still in the sun's house. The sun asks him, 'Why are you using my leggings for a pillow?' But the old man can't find an answer, he's completely confused; after all, didn't he last night run two, three miles away from the sun, and now it's morning and he is still in the sun's house. Anyway, the sun does not seem to be too troubled about the incident; he takes the leggings, folds them up and places them on his pallet. And the day passes, the sun and the old man talk about many things, about very cold weather and very hot weather, about victorious battles and losing battles, about brave men and brave animals, and they eat the deer meat that was left over from the night before. And soon it is time to go to sleep again. The old man welcomes this time, because even while he has enjoyed his long palaver with the sun, a corner of his mind has kept busy thinking about and desperately wanting those leggings.

"Anyway, it all goes as it had the night before: the sun lays down, and the instant his head touches the pallet he is asleep. The old man lays down too, and he pretends to be asleep, just in case. But finally, around midnight, he raises his head and he listens. He hears nothing; he is satisfied that the sun is deep asleep, so he tiptoes to the sun's pallet, reaches down, finds the leggings, and runs. He runs not just two or three miles, but he runs all night, runs straight as an arrow, farther and farther away from the house of the sun. At last he can run no more, and he sinks down to the ground, clutching the leggings in his arms. It seems that he has slept no more than a few minutes when he is awakened by the sun. He sits up and he looks around: this is the house of the sun! He has never left it, yet he is certain that he has not been dreaming, because his arms, his legs, his face are all scratched and bloody from his flight over rocky paths and through thick, brambly brush. His whole body aches; still, here he is in the house of the sun. And here is the sun looking down on him, asking, 'Why did you take my leggings again, this second time?' The old man mumbles something about needing a pillow.

"The sun nods and says, 'All right, if you like those leggings so well, why don't you keep them? They shall be my personal gift to you.' The old man is inflamed with joy, and, despite his weariness and many aches and bruises, he dances for the sun, waving the leggings like a flag of victory.

"There is a most powerful medicine in these leggings, the old man is well aware of that. So he decides not to use them unless he has to, to obtain food or clothing. One day his food runs out, and he searches and searches and finds nothing, and it is getting late. But there is some thick brush nearby. The old man remembers how the sun had flushed the deer from a brush like this one by using the leggings, and quickly he puts on the leggings and circles the brush, like the sun had done. Sure enough, the brush begins to burn, and several deer come leaping out. He raises his bow and takes aim—but he never fires, because the flames from the brush are spreading toward him. He turns and follows the deer, hoping they will lead him to water. He runs as fast as he can, but he's an old man, he can't keep up to the deer, he can't run as fast as the fire, and so his leggings catch fire. The leggings are of a heavy, tough material, and that protects his flesh. Luckily, he finds a creek before his flesh is badly burned. But of course the leggings have been totally destroyed. He stands in the water, shares the creek with the deer and the raccoon and the lumbering bear and beaver, all those animals that just a few minutes ago he sought to kill, and he curses the sun for ever showing him those terrible leggings. And as he curses, the animals around him begin to laugh, each one in his own voice, but each one clearly laughing."

"The sun," Tony said, "I suppose the sun stands for God."

47

"Wait. There's more to the story. Don't you want to know why the animals were laughing?"

"That's pretty obvious. They were laughing at the old man."

"No. They were laughing at the sun. They thought the sun must be pretty stupid to trust man with a gift as valuable as those leggings."

"That doesn't sound right to me."

"No, it doesn't sound right to me either," Jesse said. "That's the way Hector told it to me, but I have a suspicion that he tacked on that last part about the laughing animals."

"Well," said Tony, "I was never much of a one to believe in those fairy tales." He lifted the oars, and the boat bumped against the dock. He laid the oars on the dock and he waited for Jesse to get out so he could tie up the boat. A voice sounded over the water: "Any luck?" Both of them turned, but it was too dark to see if the voice was for them *where are they now Indians of yesteryear waters of the Flood rising out of the water staring into the sun my burden is the dead man to carry him to the shore* Tony waited. Jesse asked him: "Do you believe in God?"

"I don't not believe in him," Tony said. "But sometimes I don't very much do."

This is the sea the shore where we are sought no running this is the water I walked out of it's found me "It's hard to put your hand on," Jesse said.

"On God?" Tony asked.

"That's right."

"Do you believe?"

"That doesn't really help much, one way or the other, does it?" Jesse asked.

"Believing?"

48

Jesse stepped out of the boat, took the rope from Tony and tied up the boat. Tony followed him, and they walked off the dock, up the bank to Tony's. "Sometimes I think believing's got nothing to do with it," Jesse said. "It's enough just to be faithful."

"Whatever that means," Tony said.

"Well," Jesse said, "it's a matter of getting rid of those leggings" *walking out of the water thirteen walking* "and accepting the judgment" *that is is what it is*

"It's still just a story," Tony said.

"Yes. It's just a story. But then, that's what life's all about."

They were in front of Tony's house. "Do you want to come in?"

"No," Jesse said. "Not tonight. Maybe I got company at home."

"You know what I'd do."

"Kick 'em out."

"That's right," Tony said. "On their ear. Or worse."

"But that's not a very good way to end a story."

"To hell with the story. I'd rather save my neck."

"What's the point of it, without a good story?"

"Goodnight," Tony said.

"Goodnight." He walked away. Clouds uncovered the moon. Far away the loons called and answered, hooting *kind of laughter well so be it no leggings rising up I walk out of it into it amen*

Mrs. Laura Goodwin

My husband is not the best counselor in the world. He thinks he is the best counselor in Nortonville, but this is only because there are so few of them in Nortonville: five other pastors, a woman at the high school and two county social workers. And the truth is that Alex is probably busier than any of them; people do bring their problems to him, seven days—and seven nights—a week.

I think it is wonderful that people will trust him and confide in him. Frankly, it's one of the things that make me very proud of him. But at the same time his attitude toward counseling somehow frightens me, although I would never admit this to anyone here in Nortonville, since the difficulty may be not in his attitude, but in my understanding. Anyway, his attitude is that people can't be helped; the most that anyone can do is listen. This, of course, gives people a chance to talk, and, Alex says, the more they talk the more they realize that the listener is accepting them, and so they learn from the listener how to accept themselves and their troubles.

Once, after Alex had patiently explained this to me at considerable length, I said, "But that means we're all helpless."

And he smiled and nodded his head. "Maybe we are."

And that's what frightens me. I mean, a pastor ought to be able at least to say, "I forgive you, in the name of the Father and of the Son and of the Holy Spirit." I've never mentioned this to Alex because I suspect—I'm afraid —that he would say, "Things aren't that simple."

I say they aren't, and yet they are. It's a matter of having a rock to stand upon; it's a matter of not having to create the world all by yourself.

The story has to do with my husband. And Marie Hager and Lee Demeter. And Jesse Christian. These are the main characters. The story is about failure. I wish I could say it couldn't be helped; then maybe I could leave it behind and go on to something new. But as soon as I use the word *failure* I assume that someone was at fault, someone whose right action would have changed the situation. And perhaps that one person was my husband . . . or even I. It is in order to clear this up in my own mind that I tell the story.

It began . . . with Adam and Eve, I suppose. Marie Hager became pregnant when she was a senior in high school. The boy, the father, was Lee Demeter, a classmate of Marie's, with whom she had been going steady for almost three years. Neither Alex nor I was surprised when we heard about it from Marie's mother.

She was shocked, or at least she pretended to be. "I know they saw a lot of each other," she said, "but I thought we could trust her."

So Alex asked, "Do you think she's betrayed you?"

"Oh, I imagine it's really our fault; we shouldn't have let them see so much of each other. But what are you going to do when they insist upon it? You can't treat them like babies."

"Well," Alex went on, "what are you going to do now?"

"We . . ." Mrs. Hager stammered, "I mean, they . . . Marie just doesn't see how she can give the baby up."

"Which still doesn't answer the question of marriage," Alex said.

"Of course they'll have to get married." Of that she seemed very positive, and rather indignant that Alex would even ask the question.

But Alex, good old Alex, answered according to his custom: "There's no such thing as *having* to get married. There's no law requiring it; it's a decision you make. There are other things you could do."

"We've already considered adoption," Mrs. Hager said.

"And you've decided against it?"

"You men think adoption's the easiest way out. That's because you've never carried a baby nine months."

"Consequently we may be in a better position to make an objective decision concerning the child's future. Adoption isn't the same thing, you know, as leaving the baby on some stranger's doorstep." I hardly expected to hear that from Alex; a shrug of the shoulders or a noncommittal grunt was closer to his style. But then his next remark reassured me that it was still the same Alex.

"Any way you look at it," he said, "it's a bitter cup to swallow. Only the name of the poison is different."

But, strangely, this seemed to comfort Mrs. Hager. She nodded wearily, as if she had just been told the world was coming to an end in ten minutes. "I know it, Pastor," she said. "Indeed I know it." She sighed, dabbed at her eyes with a perfumed handkerchief, and promised to send "the children" over for a "little talk."

The next day only one of "the children" came, the father, Lee Demeter. He was one of those beautiful boys whom the whole world loves: tall, blond, shyly polite, always using "ma'am" and "sir," but also articulate, with big blue eyes and a quick smile. He was obviously intelligent, obviously graceful. One expected him to be, and he was, an excellent student, a good basketball player, and a better football player, with twelve colleges waving scholarships in his face. But there was something that worried you about Lee. I mean, he was a good boy, a golden boy really, but he seemed scared, confused, as though he had to be good and if anything damaged his perfect picture of himself, he would collapse. He had a lot of ambition; he wanted to become an urban planner.

However, his failure in family planning made this goal seem as far away as the moon. Yet, even though his situation was most embarrassing, many of his male classmates would probably have been willing to exchange places with him, to marry the luscious Miss Hager and thus fall heir to the sizable estate and social prestige of the Hagers. Mr. Hager was a realtor who did as much buying as he did selling, until most of his time was spent in collecting rent and investing in mutual funds. Any son-in-law of August Hager could look forward to any one of several pleasing prospects: managing a large farm, running a theater or a men's clothing store, or acting as junior partner and errand-boy for August. For Lee these were all far less rigorous alternatives than going to college, since his parents (Lee's father worked in the shipping department at the Nortonville Creamery) would be unable to give him any financial support.

Nevertheless, he said No to the marriage. He and Alex were together for over an hour; they must have talked about a lot of things, but all Alex told me was that Lee still planned to go to college, that he felt sorry for Marie, that he loved her but was simply not ready to settle down as a husband *and* a father. Apparently, he was not angry or defensive about it; he had made up his mind, that was all. And after he had talked to Alex, he went to see the Hagers, to tell them of his decision.

That same week, Clifford Demeter, Lee's father, lost his job at the creamery—maybe not coincidentally, for August Hager was chairman of the board of directors. Anyway, the superintendent claimed that Mr. Demeter had been drinking on the job—and this was quite possible; Clifford Demeter had in fact frequently been drunk on the job, but it was not a complicated job and, drunk or sober, he worked hard. But sometimes when he was drunk he lost his temper and did things he regretted; people mostly forgot about those times. Of course, now there was a new factor to consider, an unborn baby who was already meddling in other people's lives.

Mr. Demeter was obviously unable to strike back at the unborn child, so instead he threw Lee out of the house. From this point on, I am strictly an observer—actually, not even that: I've heard several stories about what happened, and now I'm piecing them together, keeping in mind what I know firsthand. Anyway, Lee went to Jesse Christian's place, I suppose because he and Jesse had often gone fishing together. But more than that, Lee had become somewhat of an outcast, a moral infidel, and he probably suspected that Jesse's was the one place where he would fit in. Because Jesse was not exactly the first citizen of Nortonville.

Of course Jesse took him in. No doubt Lee simply knocked on the door and asked if he could stay for a while. And no doubt Jesse simply said Yes, you're welcome. It's hard to imagine that it was much more complicated or elaborate than that. But I did hear that Jesse later on tried to persuade Lee to go home, and then to talk things over with Marie. If so, it didn't work; Lee didn't go home. But he did see Marie, a few days after he moved in with Jesse. People saw them on the river road; Marie was driving her father's car and Lee was sitting beside her.

Whatever they said was their business, and so it remains. All I know is that the next night, shortly before midnight, Marie Hager was taken to the hospital. Some say she tried to commit suicide and that she used benzedrine, aspirin, strychnine: take your choice. Others say she was only interested in aborting the baby. All I ever heard for certain was that she lost the baby. And, since she was hospitalized for a long time with a serious infection which rendered her sterile (again, hearsay), I suspect that that's all she really wanted to do: lose the baby. No, that isn't quite true, either. What she really wanted to do was return to . . . innocence, I suppose. And the trouble is that the harder you work to become innocent, usually the more and more guilt you incur—you just get more deeply involved. It's better to see your guilt through and not run away from it. But that advice is cheap, even if it is true. The fact is that what she did, my husband reminds me, was to murder her baby.

However, my husband never really went out of his way to tell other people this. Most other people weren't ready to hear it: nice girls from nice families don't do that sort of thing. So it had to be Lee's fault, Lee's insistence, Lee's advice, Lee's assistance. But after all, Lee Demeter was an all-American boy. And all-American boys don't do that sort of thing, either. So, finally, it had to be Jesse Christian's fault. Because he was an outsider. And since abortion and—well, murder—were foreign ideas,

55

events that didn't belong in Nortonville, he was the only person who could have brought them in. It was he who had infected Lee Demeter, who had subsequently poisoned—literally and figuratively—the lovely, innocent Marie Hager. Certainly this was far easier to believe than the preposterous notion that little Marie, the Eve in our Garden, should bear the guilt all by herself.

Anyway, it was a grand week for the town gossips. "Her life is ruined, that's all there is to it!" Some of them said it with a kind of glee. It made me want to shout, Vengeance is *mine,* says the Lord. But for the Hagers it was a time to retreat, regroup, and prepare for attack.

The rest is behind closed doors and after dark. For that reason, I can put it down in relatively few words. Yet I am afraid that those few words will be wholly unequal to the need I feel to give an accurate name to the nameless horror of it. I mean, I could go on for pages and pages, talking about the puny insinuations and the smirking hypocrisies aimed at those two who *"seemed* to be such a nice young couple." There is something very dirty about these finger-pointing, sex-ridden chatterers—still, their sin is actually a refusal to face up to the real, low-down dirt: they want to identify evil with the passion of sex so they won't have to look into those nether dimensions of death and disobedience. Not that I am so very morally courageous; I would prefer to talk about the evils of premarital intercourse and let it go at that. But something more is involved, something far more frightening than the thought or act of two teen-agers learning how to make love.

On a Sunday afternoon about two weeks after her abortion, Marie Hager was still in the hospital, still in "critical condition," when two men visited Jesse Christian. They beat him, using tire chains. The chains flecked with his blood were found on the kitchen floor. Miraculously, not a single bone was broken. But his eyes were swollen shut, one ear was almost torn off, and his legs and back (so I heard from the nurses at the hospital) were one massive bloody bruise. He had also been clouted on the back of his head with a heavy, blunt instrument. Apparently, it all happened in his kitchen. Whoever it was had been let in by Jesse; then, when his back was turned, they hit him.

He was found in the evening by Tony Sauer's wife. Tony took him to the hospital, and there he lay unconscious for three days. Tony was his only visitor. I told Alex that a pastor should be there, too. But Alex felt that if he went he would be insulting the Hagers, and thus would be in no position to help the Hagers and Lee Demeter settle their problems. Perhaps he was right; at least, it made sense. But as it turned out neither the Hagers nor Lee Demeter ever came to see Alex, and, even though he went regularly to see Marie in the hospital, no one ever mentioned the aborted baby or Lee Demeter—or Jesse Christian.

Jesse was released from the hospital on the same day that Marie's high fever broke and she was taken off the critical list. Tony Sauer and his wife took Jesse home, and they nursed him there. Not too many days later, Marie went home. Now she's a college student, in California, I think. I doubt that she's been home since she enrolled; I doubt that she will come home again, although her parents fly out regularly to see her.

Clifford Demeter has his job back again. And Lee Demeter is attending the state university. He looks every inch the college man, immaculately dressed, more polished now than when he left Nortonville, and less shy. He is doing very well, so I am told.

There are now other things to talk about, other instances of pregnancy out of wedlock and adultery and divorce. Yet the Hager affair is hardly forgotten; people continue to derive a certain pleasure from reconstructing it. And every time this is done, there is always one person who will suggest that August Hager paid somebody a handsome sum to have Jesse Christian thrashed, not merely to teach Jesse a lesson but to stress that Jesse was the real villain. And that villainy does not go unpunished in a God-fearing community.

Someone else, then, will intimate that those who beat Jesse at August's orders were not strangers to Jesse Christian, that, indeed, one of them may even have been living with Jesse at the time. After all, there was evidence that Jesse welcomed them into his home and that he trusted them enough to turn his back on them.

But of course Jesse welcomed everyone into his home, friends and strangers alike. The fact that he was hit on the back of the head and not on the front proves nothing.

Still, Lee Demeter is going to college, and he seems to have an unusual amount of spending money, more than his father could possibly give him. But Lee Demeter is such a nice young boy, hardworking and bright, with real ambition and high goals—he wouldn't consider doing such a thing.

What's really meant is that no one who talks about it wants to consider it: *it* being the idea that a fine Christian gentleman, August Hager, would coolly draw up a no-nonsense dollars-and-cents contract to have a man beaten up and, possibly, murdered; *it* being the further implication that a clean-cut, likable young man, Lee Demeter, would coolly sign the contract and proceed to deliver the goods. The beating itself has never been a matter of particular concern; it may have been a bit crude, but Jesse did recover. And his silence concerning the identity of his attackers has made him seem considerably less than an innocent victim. No, the consensus is that he got what was coming to him. But if it was at the hands of Lee Demeter and at the urging of August Hager, then whatever common conscience there is in this town, whatever sense of propriety, whatever image of shared goodness and decency, is blackened by this candlelit scene in which the Good Man and the Beautiful Boy smile gangsterlike at one another, and each one sells his soul for blood. If they could do that, no man is safe from his neighbor.

As for what I believe . . . well, practically every Sunday, except when they're in California, I see the Hagers in church; on occasion, I've knelt next to them for Holy Communion. I desperately do not want to believe that August Hager was involved in the beating. Because if he was, that splendid decency of his would be nothing but a mask. It isn't that I mind masks; I wear them myself, who doesn't? But there has to be some connection, something that all the masks have in common. I mean, a mask ought to reveal, it ought to tell at least a little bit of the truth about the person who's wearing it. But what kind of truth could that mask of decency reveal if August Hager had once peeled off a roll of bills to have a man tortured almost to death?

But that isn't all. There's another side of the story. This is to accept that August Hager instigated the beating of Jesse Christian (as far as I know, he's never denied it), but that he did it as a heroic preserver of our best traditions. (Now this is all Alex's point of view, not mine; in fact, I don't care much for it, although I do admire Alex's ingenuity and admit that it makes sense.) From this point of view, what was at stake was our community's confidence in marriage and in the correctness of our understanding of marriage. We go along with a little hypocrisy, but only a little. On the surface, we say: no premarital intercourse, no extramarital intercourse; first marriage, then sex, and then children. And this isn't just a matter of being moralistic; it means respecting the family, preserving the family, saying over and over again that even though all families are not good families, the family is still a pretty good institution. At the same time, we can absorb infractions of the rules; we are not too shocked when we hear about girls like Marie getting pregnant; the misery and shame are punishment enough and signs, too, that this is not the best way. The parents all agree: "If they had only waited." They support marriage and the family. And then they do what they can to fit their pregnant little girl into that picture of marriage and the family. In other words, they try to get her married. Or else they send her away, pretending that the baby is some kind of tumor that must be removed and given away before the girl can present herself in the community again.

I know it doesn't always work out in precisely those ways. But the point is that we feel it is right and proper to honor marriage and the family even when, *particularly* when, we have cheated on marriage and the family. Because we wouldn't want the cheating to become the normal thing to do. We are all wise enough to know that there will always be cheating of some kind, there will always be disobedience. But this is all the more reason to insist that cheating not become identified with right action. If that were ever to happen, then everything would be right, nothing would be wrong, and no one would know where he stood; all would be chaos.

So what was *really* wrong, then, was not Lee and Marie's lovemaking or her pregnancy. It was the idea that she could get rid of the baby whenever she wanted to. When you go against the traditions of marriage and the family you run the risk of getting caught, and if you are caught you pay the price. And if you pay graciously and make a good confession, you're reinstated in the community as a member in good standing again. But if you try to get out of paying, if you turn your back on marriage and the family, then the community has to get tough. It's a matter of self-preservation.

But this time was different: August Hager could not be expected to "get tough" with his own daughter, so he brought in Jesse Christian, he made Jesse pay.

According to this notion Alex has, there aren't any villains, and the hero, August Hager, is not exactly heroic. The community, along with our need for law and order and for knowing right from wrong, is in the center. And in order to preserve the community's sanctity, or sanity, or maybe both, certain leaders have to play the role of judge, whether they like it or not. And certain people have to be punished, not necessarily because of what they have done, but because they stand for a kind of lawlessness that the community cannot abide. August Hager the judge punishes Jesse Christian the scapegoat. It's nothing personal, it's an emphasizing of our law and order: our sexual experiences are contained, our children are conceived and born and raised within the confines of marriage and the family. There may be better ways of doing things, but for the time being this is the best way we know.

And so I ask Alex: "What about compassion? What about forgiveness?"

"That's up to Jesse Christian," Alex says. "Don't expect

August Hager to know anything about that. His business is the law."

"You're being terribly old-fashioned, aren't you?" I say.

"All I'm saying is that you can't have a community without certain prearranged, generally agreed-upon laws and customs." He pauses for a moment. "And since sex and conception and birth are so terribly basic to the continuance of the community, you can't expect that there won't be laws and customs centering around sex and conception and birth."

Alex makes sense, and I admit this. Then I ask: "Isn't there some way to make laws and customs about forgiveness? Can't you fit that into your legislation, too?"

He doesn't answer right away. Finally he says: "Ask Jesse Christian." He crosses the room and looks out the window, his back toward me. "He took the boy in, he absorbed a beating from this same boy, he said nothing—he absorbed—so that whatever guilt fell upon Lee Demeter and Marie Hager when they broke our laws and customs was whipped into Jesse by those tire chains. And now the laws still stand, and so, I suppose, do the scars on his back, and the loneliness too, because none of us cared to visit him, to see the guilt we had all unloaded upon his back. No, you ask him about forgiveness."

"Maybe August Hager should ask him," I say.

Alex turns from the window and looks at me. "Maybe he already has," he says.

"Maybe he should," I say.

"Maybe he has," Alex repeats. And I let the subject rest.

The Reverend Alex Goodwin

No one in Nortonville will ever, or should ever, completely forget that tangled mess of useless passion that began so promisingly but ended, in mere exhaustion, in Marie Hager's abortion and Jesse Christian's beating. It was two outbursts of violence—and it meant nothing at all; there was nothing to show for it, nothing to point to. So even if people will always remember the incident for its violence, it has already (barely a year later) become transparent: not to be forgotten, true, but still just a matter for the mind, and nothing for the eye to see.

Now a cyclone would have been different; it would have left visible scars, something amounting to landmarks, a mangled piece of steel or a broken brick you could lift in your hand and say, "This is where the twister went and this is what she left."

But Jesse Christian's scars, if he received any lasting ones, are covered by his shirt; besides, he only rarely comes into town. Marie Hager's scars are all internal—the worst kind, I suppose, yet the kind that are easiest for the rest of us to put aside. And, of course, Marie is away from us; so is Lee Demeter.

That leaves August Hager, who is no more and no less prominent than he has always been. He still attends church regularly, he plays golf every Thursday afternoon in the summer, he is at almost every Rotary luncheon on Wednesday noons, and there have been rumors around town that he is being asked to run for a seat on the local school board next fall.

Frankly, he makes me uneasy, and I am ashamed of myself that I did not minister to him more forthrightly while Marie was in the hospital. At that time I expressed my regrets, I hoped that all would go well; all in all, I think I made him as uncomfortable as he made me. The trouble is that August Hager never seems to look back; at least, while Marie was entering her own little Calvary, he was plotting ahead, engaged in molding the future, accepting the present as a case of temporary bad luck but determined to turn this bad luck into a happy ending strictly through his own energy. And heaven knows he had, he *has*, energy. He started out in Nortonville as a hulking high school dropout whose father wanted him to work on the family farm. But at sixteen August Hager had other ideas, so he left home and took a job as an office boy and all-around handyman for Jonathan Cartwright, a cranky insurance man who was looking for slave labor. He gave August five dollars a week and a room in the basement of his office building. In turn, August gave Cartwright twelve to fifteen hours a day, filing policies, sending bills, typing letters (he had to learn that skill on his own time), stoking the office furnace, mowing Cartwright's lawn, planting Cartwright's roses, and soothing Cartwright's rheumatism with oil-of-eucalyptus backrubs.

Everyone in Nortonville said he was a fool, behind his back. But August kept working, listening, learning how to be polite and when to be firm. And nine years later, after Cartwright finally died at seventy-seven, shouting at the nurses that his checkbook wouldn't balance and cursing August for juggling his account books and embezzling millions—after all of that, August, who never cheated but still managed to save ten dollars a month, took over the business. Because he was there. And it was all in black and white. Cartwright's will, like his person, was sharp and uncomplicated: the business (building, clients and all outstanding debts) went to August. The house was to be sold at auction and the proceeds added to the estate—four hundred and eighty thousand dollars in cash, stocks and bonds, and a dozen or so mortgages. The estate was to be divided equally among the four churches in the community, provided that one Sunday each year would be set aside as Jonathan P. Cartwright Memorial Sunday, on which day the pastor would preach a sermon in praise of thrift and perseverance and, not incidentally, the benevolence of one Jonathan P. Cartwright.

The Baptist and the Catholic churches turned down the offer; the Methodist and Lutheran churches accepted. I don't know why the Methodists agreed, but August explained the Lutheran position shortly after I became the pastor here. First of all, it was simply good business, he said. And then he had reminded the deacons of the church that the will did not stipulate the date or the hour of the service. So, to this day, and forevermore, the date is the last Sunday in July, and the time of the service is 4:30 A.M. And for the past six years, on the last Sunday in July, I have mounted to the pulpit and read: "We hereby commend Jonathan P. Cartwright for his thrift and good will in behalf of the Church, the Body of Christ. May this gift be of service in endowing the Church with a spirit of faithful commitment to her Lord and Savior. Amen." Then the lone member in the congregation, August Hager, repeats the Amen, and we go to the parsonage for coffee. And then August usually goes fishing, since he figures that he's been to church for that day.

Once I asked August if he attended merely to check up on me. "No," he said. "It's the least I can do for the old devil." He seemed embarrassed at having used that last word in front of a preacher, so he explained: "I worked for what I got, but just the same he didn't have to give it to me. That means that I don't have to be grateful, don't have to be grateful at all. But just the same, I am."

"It's the same way between God and man," I said.

"Well, maybe," he said. "I never thought of it that way, though."

"God doesn't *have* to give us anything, either," I said.

"Well, I don't know," August said. "It seems to me that it isn't quite right to compare God and old man Cartwright. It doesn't seem likely that anybody's going to improve on what God does, but if I do say so myself, I think I've improved quite a bit on what Cartwright did."

"Even on the four hundred and eighty thousand dollars?"

"He was seventy-seven before he got that far," August said solemnly. "I'm only fifty-three."

That was three years ago; now August Hager is three years closer to seventy-seven and three years closer to four hundred and eighty thousand dollars. Not that I believe he'll ever reach that sum; taxes would help to prevent him, but so would his method of operation. He doesn't handle insurance anymore, for example, because, someone told me, he isn't interested in turning over less than a thousand dollars in any single deal (none of this "a penny saved is a penny earned" business). He simply roams the country, letting one transaction lead him to another, going from

66

state to state, buying a farm, selling or trading it for an office building, going from there into cattle or oil wells. I have heard that he has two lawyers working for him full time to keep his dealings straight.

Of course I have also heard that if he were forced to liquidate tomorrow he would have to go into bankruptcy. In other words, he has thousands of dollars at his disposal, but nothing in the bank. Somehow this is more impressive than if he had his safe-deposit box stuffed with thousand dollar bills (as did Cartwright). August Hager makes money work for him; he plows under dollar bills, and five dollar bills grow up; he harvests five dollar bills and sells them for tens; he invests the tens and they return as twenties. And always there is activity, a restless experimentation in the multiplication of money, not in order to *have,* to accumulate money, but in order to *make,* to create.

It is difficult, for me at least, to talk to this kind of man about another Creator. But one day he came to me (I have never been more surprised in all my life) to talk about a redeemer.

Well, it wasn't as obvious or clear-cut as that. He came to the parsonage one night several weeks ago; he didn't waste time with the weather or the latest baseball scores, he came right out, before he'd even sat down, and said: "I've been thinking about that fellow who got roughed up . . . while Marie was in the hospital."

"Jesse Christian."

"Do you know who did it?"

"I have my ideas," I said. "I suppose everyone in town has ideas."

"It was a hellish experience," he said. "And it doesn't seem to get any better."

"But it was only six months ago," I said. "Those things take time. She's all right now, isn't she?"

"Marie?" he asked.

"Isn't that who you meant?"

"I meant both of them."

"Jesse Christian, too?"

"The boy did it . . . and his father. You won't tell anybody, will you?"

"No," I said. "What good would it do?"

"I don't say he didn't have it coming," August said. "He should have sent the boy home instead of letting him stay out there."

"Maybe he thought he was doing the right thing."

"I did too," he said, slowly, angrily. "I did too, when I arranged to have those two go out and beat him up."

"And now what?"

"I went out to see him last night. We talked things over." The angry tone was gone from his voice; now he spoke as a man who had just talked over a deal to buy a carload of wheat. "He's a reasonable man."

And then, because I felt it was obscene to bring in the matter of reasonableness in talking about a man whom you had had beaten almost to death. I blurted out: "You didn't try to pay him off, too, did you?"

And he shouted at me, "Yes, I was going to pay him off, too. Do you think that was dirty?"

"Did you think that would erase the suffering you put him through?" I shouted back. "Or were you afraid he'd talk?"

"If I'd been afraid of that," he said, "I would have gone to him while he was still in the hospital. I'm not afraid of consequences. But I thought I owed him something."

"What would that be?"

"I wasn't fair."

"You tried to play God."

"All right. If that's the way you want to put it."

"And what do you want from me?"

"He told me to come to you. . . ." And then the un-loosing of August Hager's burden. He sat back and spoke softly—I had to lean forward to catch the words . . . not really a confession, not a conversation, rather a statement: This is who I am.

"I wasn't fair," he said. "But you understand that I had to do something, I couldn't sit still and not do something after what happened to Marie. And I couldn't do anything to the boy. I went after his father, but as soon as I did that I realized it was . . . petty, foolish. Like a . . . a bull stampeding after a fly. So Christian seemed like the natural one: he was as guilty as anyone. Not for what he did so much as for what he was. I mean, he didn't belong here, he wasn't one of us.

"That isn't fair, is it? To say that. He has his rights. And like you say, I'm not God. But just the same, you can't watch your daughter go through hell and not do something about it.

"So, to tell the truth, I'm not sorry for him. But I should have done it myself, I shouldn't have sent that boy and his drunkard father to do my work for me. Because they weren't good enough for him. Do you know what I mean? They went because they were paid—and I suppose that, as far as they were concerned, they would rather have been whipping me than him. I know I'm not loved. That's your business, after all. You're getting paid to love and to be loved.

"And my business . . . well, my business is to keep things running the way they always have been. Sure, nobody appointed me to the job, but, I guarantee you, they expect it from me. It would be easier for my business if I moved to Minneapolis, or Omaha, or Denver. But if I left, the people like Clifford Demeter would take over—soon, there'd be no one left but people like Clifford Demeter. And people like you—only you wouldn't have the hardness to deal with Clifford Demeter. And neither does Jesse Christian. I blame him for opening his door to young Demeter—nothing else. But that was enough, because it gave Demeter, and Marie too, the idea that whenever authority, genuine authority, put its foot down, there would be someplace to run, someplace to hide.

"And that's what people like me are for: we're here to make it plain to people like Clifford Demeter that there aren't any places to hide from authority. I have old man Cartwright to thank for teaching me that. My father never did, never thought of it, because he ran as much as anybody: when my mother got after him about not having enough money, he ran into the barn; when he saw that the barn needed new shingles or just a simple cleaning, he ran into town. But with Cartwright there wasn't any of that, there wasn't a single free minute, and after a few years I learned to appreciate it. I knew where I stood with Cartwright: always under orders, always responsible. And love had nothing to do with it; I never loved Cartwright and he never loved me, and I'm not sure there was any great respect, either. But there was order; the bills were sent out on time, and there was coal in the furnace, and at the end of the month the books balanced.

"And now this business happens. And the fact remains that I was not fair. I didn't intend it that way. But I didn't think it out as carefully as I should have. And it bothered me. So finally I went to see him.

"I went at night. Because I was ashamed. And I was ashamed of being ashamed. That's the truth, and I hate to admit it; I was ashamed of going to see him, and going after dark only added to it. Anyway, I did go.

"I found him in his kitchen. I knocked on the door and this voice—I expected it would be deeper and louder, but it was high-pitched and kind of singsongy—well, he asked me to come in . . . without knowing who I was, but knowing that there could be trouble, that there had been once before. I walked in and saw him eating supper; I suppose it was supper, a bowl of corn flakes and a cup of coffee. When he saw me, he nodded and got up and motioned me to sit down at the table with him. Then he poured me a cup of coffee.

"I asked him if he knew who I was, and he nodded that he did. Then I asked how he was feeling, and he said that he was fine, and then he said: 'I'd given up on you.'

" 'What do you mean?' I asked.

" 'Just what I said,' he replied.

" 'Did they tell you?' I asked him.

" 'Nobody told me anything,' he said. 'I'm only guessing.'

" 'You're right,' I said.

" 'I suppose you had your reasons,' he said.

" 'I had reasons,' I told him.

" 'It was too bad,' he said. And then he added: 'For both of us.'

"I didn't answer him, I just sat back and drank my coffee and looked at him—it was the first time I had ever really looked at him from close up. He isn't a very big man, but he moves quick and he's very muscular. If he had fought back, those two would have had a hard time with him. I couldn't figure it out, either he didn't fight back or else they hit him first from behind. Either way . . . well, I didn't go into that; I knew all I needed to know, and if he wanted to tell me more, that was his business.

" 'You don't want to apologize, do you?' he asked.

" 'No,' I said. 'Not exactly.'

" 'I didn't think so,' he said.

"And right then and there I knew that I couldn't offer him the money I had in my pocket. It was a good sum too, enough to keep him comfortable for quite a few months. I couldn't offer it to him—I don't think he would have accepted it in the first place—but if I had offered it, it wouldn't have settled anything. Money talks to people like the Demeters, but it doesn't talk *for* people, it doesn't explain anything. So I guess there just comes a time when you have to sit down, face to face, and say what you think and listen. I told him that I hadn't been fair to him.

"And he asked, 'Is that all?'

" 'No,' I answered, 'that isn't all. You see, I got involved with you, not because I wanted to, but because that's the way things worked out. I thought I could handle the whole matter without having to see you.'

"He said to me, 'You thought that once you had paid them you could forget about it.'

"And I said, 'That's more or less what I thought.'

"Then he said what I had known all along, that I was disgusted with myself. I was disgusted with myself because those Demeters made me disgusted—so help me God, I'm a better man than they'll ever be—and still I'm the one who turned those two loose like dogs on that man. I knew what they would do (at least, I knew what the old man would do), and I set them loose to do it. Once they spend the money, they'll be back in harness again. Maybe the boy will amount to something. I hope so. But what I'm talking about is that I'm still loose: I didn't get any money; I didn't get the satisfaction of hitting him—I mean Jesse Christian—across the back with those chains until my arms ached; I didn't get anything out of it, except the knowledge that not only did I have a man beat up who probably deserved it, but I also made a bad man worse and a boy who was only stupid, well, I made him guilty.

"And I'm a good man. How can a good man do such terrible things?

"He said to me, 'My wounds are all healed.'

" 'I don't know about mine,' I replied. 'I don't even know if I've got any.'

"And he said, 'That's hard to know.' Then he poured some more coffee, and we sat there and we drank and neither one of us said anything for what seemed like a long time.

"Finally he looked at me, and he said, 'Mr. Hager, the thing you deserve most is death.'

"He said it in the same tone of voice that you might use to ask for a box of cough drops. And I honestly expected that the next thing he would do would be to pull out a gun and let me have it. But instead he asked me, 'What do you think you deserve?' And the funny thing is that I'd never thought about that before, but right on the spot I could see that I pretty well didn't deserve the best.

" 'I know I'm not perfect,' I said to him. But at least I thought I deserved to be left alone, to mind my own business, and I was going to say just that when I realized that of course I have never left other people alone—I don't apologize for it—I have simply accepted responsibility, and I suppose that is a kind of meddling in other people's business, and not always for the best, either.

" 'Maybe you're right,' I said.

" 'I could hound you to death, you know,' he said. 'I could follow you around town, stand outside your house, sit behind you in church like some silent black angel.'

" 'I'd have you arrested as a public nuisance,' I said.

" 'And you could have it done, too,' he said.

" 'You bet I could have it done,' I said.

" 'There would have to be a trial,' he said. 'And you would have to testify.'

" 'It might be a pleasure,' I said.

" 'Only if you could be strictly a spectator,' he said.

"And of course that would be a luxury for me. The only time I ever feel like a spectator is when I'm sitting in church—until the collection plate comes around.

"Anyway, I had to admit that it wouldn't be much of a pleasure to see him tried as a public nuisance. And then I told him I certainly wasn't angry with him, and I never had been; it wasn't anything personal.

"But he said, 'I've made it personal—and maybe you couldn't help letting it become personal, either, since you did know my name from the beginning, and so sooner or later you had to come and see me, to find out if I really existed or if I was only a name. You had me attacked, and you wanted to see if it was real honest-to-goodness flesh and blood that got kicked and cut up. Well, it was. Do you want to see the scars? Do you want to feel them? They belong to you, after all—I'm only bearing them for the time being, until you can take over, if that day ever comes.'

"I told him that kind of talk was all nonsense. And he smiled, and I thought that under different conditions I might have liked the man. As it was, I didn't know whether to dislike him or to be afraid of him, afraid because I didn't know exactly how to take the man. So I asked him then and there to lay his cards on the table.

" 'All right,' he said. 'The truth is that I bother you; you don't know what to do with me; you tried violence and that didn't work, and you doubt that money will work, either. Well, you're simply going to have to accept that I'm part of your world, a kind of brother under the skin who takes the beatings that you deserve.

" 'And I don't feel sorry for you. And I don't despise you. And I'm not disgusted with you. At least you're *concerned* about being just.'

"I thought he was trying to mock me, and I told him so. And he said to me that I wasn't used to being mocked, was I? 'No,' I said, 'I'm not. I'm a respectable person.'

" 'Well,' he said, 'I'm used to it, I'm used to it all the time. And do you know something? It makes more sense than respectability.'

" 'That depends on what you mean by *sense*,' I said.

"Then he said that he had probably used the wrong word, because what he really meant was that everybody should have a kind of worm's-eye view of himself. He said it's like the time that Eve took the apple and raised it to her lips to take that first bite, and the worm peeked out and said, 'Now we're on the same level.'

"It's a funny little story, but I'm not sure what it has to do with me. That's what I told him. And then he said:

" 'Don't you see, I'm the worm in your apple. Of course it isn't quite as simple as all that.' He was smiling and leaning over the table, like some kind of madman. I don't know why I listened to him, now that I look back on it, I don't know. But I remember that at the time . . . well, everything fit together. He said that the world is my apple.

" 'And you keep shining it and polishing it,' he said. 'But then you take a closer look and you see you've got some bruises and some soft spots on your beautiful red apple. What you've got on your hands is really a decaying apple, a red, ripe, juicy, decaying apple. But of course that's the way apples are, even the best apples: they don't stay perfect forever. And no matter how careful you are, they get old and they get spoiled. So you wonder if you shouldn't just cut out the bad places, but you try that, and pretty soon the nice, clean white spots turn brown. At last you look, and there's the final worm grinning at you, and you can't cut him out because he's wrapped himself all through the apple.

" 'That's your world, Mr. Hager,' he said to me. 'That's your world, and I'm the worm. And I'm here to tell you that even if you helped to spoil this apple, there'll be other ones, other chances. And the other worms you're bound to find, Mr. Hager—remember me when you find them— they're meant to mock you, to remind you that you picked the apple, you didn't make it. So whatever you get—remember that I'm the worm—whatever you get is grace.'

"I told him that was ridiculous. 'Whatever you get is grace.' I don't think so. I don't think that what happened to Marie was grace. And I told him that, too.

"He stopped smiling. 'I know what you mean,' he said. 'I wish I could offer you some sort of explanation.'

"And then I said something I never expected to say: 'I wish,' I said, 'I wish I could offer you an easy explanation.'

" 'You bit into the worm,' he said, 'And you got the bad taste in your mouth. And you were surprised, too, that a worm could be living in your apple.'

" 'Stop talking about that,' I said.

" 'All right,' he said. 'Let's just say that I was cut in two, and I was healed. And now I pronounce you healed, too. And that's that. Would you like some more coffee— maybe something a little stronger in it?'

"I said I would. He put something in it, brandy I think. And we drank it, and he asked me how Marie was getting along. And I told him she was getting along fine. He said he was glad to hear it. We finished drinking, and I left.

"Now all day long I've been wanting to tell somebody about it. And I thought you would probably understand as well as anybody in town. It's just that I feel like a different man. And now I've told you. And I suppose you'll keep it under your hat."

I assured him that I would. He shook my hand, and he left. I've kept my word; I haven't even told my wife, who, luckily, was not at home that evening. I see August Hager regularly; that is, almost every Sunday and occasionally on the street. But we never mention our conversation; I don't think we ever will.

The strange thing is that ordinarily when someone makes a confession the person who listens is tempted, even though he doesn't want to be, to feel a kind of superiority over the one who confesses. On the surface, at least, it would seem fairly normal—to feel, I mean, that I have a moral edge on August Hager, who came to me in weakness to tell me how he had been leveled by an outsider. But the fact is that August Hager has grown, in my eyes, by coming to grips with the demon under his skin and by forcing this demon to stand outside, naked, in the presence of his innocent victim. It's a rare experience, requiring a kind of courage that no curriculum can teach. I envy the man. And I envy Jesse Christian, too, who was willing to spread a feast in the presence of his enemy.

And I marvel how close together are heaven and hell, the demonic and the holy. I spend my days going around saying nice things to nice people, making myself generally decent and kind; I try not to offend, I want to be reasonably well-liked. Deep down, I have stirrings of viciousness, a desire to smash the world I live in for no reason other than that it does not seem to me to be the best of all possible worlds; I suspect that as creator I could have done a better job than was done. Sometimes I feel I would like to lay all these things on the line, to look somebody straight in the eye and say exactly what I feel and think, to let out all of the poison and fear within me. But I don't know how; I feel bottled up, there are tons of energy boiling inside—so I spend my time swatting flies and driving too fast when I'm sure there are no police nearby.

August Hager went to see Jesse Christian: the hunter laid down his arms and put his life in his victim's hands. And he was right, he did become a new man, he was healed.

Tony Sauer

—Testing . . . one . . . two . . . three . . . one . . . two . . . three. . . . My name is Kurt Farris, and I'm an English teacher at Nortonville High School. The other voice you will hear is that of Tony Sauer, owner of a Nortonville resort. The date is April 30, 1962.

—And I just talk into that little microphone?

—That's right, Tony.

—And you just want me to tell what happened?

—On and around March 6, 1962.

—Well, it doesn't make much difference to me; still, it seems like it's too late for this kind of thing to do anybody any good.

—I thought we'd settled that. I don't know if this is going to do anybody any *good*. But maybe someday somebody will wonder why this all had to happen, or maybe someday it will be about to happen again, and then the people here will have these recordings to listen to, and that might be enough to persuade them not to.

—Not to what?

—Not to become animals.

—What's happened once can happen again. And nothing I got to say's going to change that.

—Then do it for his sake.

—That's who I am doing it for. Once he said we ought to be as smart as serpents. . . .

—Wise. 'Wise as serpents and innocent as doves.' It's from the Bible.

—Anyway, I said you couldn't be both. And he said you had to be if you wanted to do anybody any good. You had to be smarter than all the snakes in the grass that keep trying to sting you; you got to know all their secrets. And at the same time, you can't use their methods. Or else you just become another snake.

—What happened on March 6th?

—Well, I always said Jesse was a fool to do it, because you can never tell what some of these kids will do. They're wild and they run away from home and they figure they've got nothing to lose. But Jesse took them in.

It started about seven, eight years ago. I remember it was just before his barn burned down. These two Indian boys, about twelve, thirteen years old, they sneaked into his barn one night and he caught them. They was from the Twin Pine Reservation up in Harding County and they was just wandering through the country since there was no school and they had about ten brothers and sisters and never enough food and never a decent place to sleep anyway, so they figured if they had to go hungry they might as well have a little adventure with it. And when they got down into Clinton County somehow they heard about Jesse, and they had never before seen a real live Negro, so they made it over here to see if he was anything like an Indian. Funny thing was that they thought he looked more like a white man than an Indian. And Jesse said with a big wink that it was nice of them to say so.

I mean, he was always real polite that way, and as soon as he saw that these two were just plain curious about the world outside Twin Pine, he told them they could stay as long as they liked—that is, until school started.

Of course, I don't think Jesse was an educated man. He never told me much about it, but I am pretty certain he never finished high school. Once I asked him what he was doing up here, and he turned around and asked me the same.

'I guess it's that I like to fish,' I said. 'Fishing don't hurt nobody.'

'The trouble is,' he said, 'that in a lot of places there are more laws to protect fish than there are for people.' We was sitting by the lake and he started throwing pebbles into it, little pebbles, one at a time. 'Those are people,' he said. 'This one starved to death. And that one got shot. And this one jumped off a bridge. And that one burned. And this one just cried himself to death.' Then he scooped up the pebbles with both hands and he said, 'Maybe that's what I'm here for, to learn how to be a people conservationist.' And he laid down the pebbles very gently, like they were some kind of living creatures.

Anyway, like I was saying, Jesse's barn was burned down —which is another story, except that after it happened Jesse said that it was only the beginning, like sharks when they first taste blood in the water. I said that about the sharks, and Jesse said, 'Maybe so. But I am not going to wait for them, sharks or whatever they are, I am not going to wait for them to come here. I am going up to them.' At the time I did not know what Jesse meant, and he did not offer any explanation. At the time we thought—at least, I thought—that the Indian boys were the ones that those kids from town were after, with the help of Howard Willson and heaven knows how many other "respectable" people. The Indian boys thought they was the targets, too, and they broke for home before the sun came up the next morning. And Jesse said, 'Well, that's the end of the Indians.'

But it wasn't the end of them at all. I suppose the farther they got away from Nortonville the less scared they were and the more exciting the barn-burning seemed. And by the time they got home, well, it was one big lark. So it got to be a regular thing that every two, three months a handful of ragged Sioux boys would traipse onto Jesse's property, usually end up in the barn, and, when he discovered them, say to him, 'You Christian?' And he'd nod and fix them oatmeal and eggs.

Sometimes they'd sneak away in the middle of the night. Most of the time they'd wait until midmorning, because Jesse made it a habit to fix them sandwiches to take along on their trip back home—it was about one-fifty, one-sixty miles, and I expect they walked most of the way. Or ran. That's one thing an Indian can do is run, especially if he's getting chased. And I don't necessarily mean chased for stealing, but mostly chased just for being an Indian and being in the way of the white man's civilization. 'The triumph of streetcars and syphilis,' Jesse said.

But I told him I didn't think that was exactly fair. And he said that he knew it wasn't. Then he'd tell that story from the Bible about the Israelites wanting a king and Samuel telling them that God was their king and he should be enough—and besides a human king would collect taxes and build up an army. Still, that is what the people wanted, so that is what they got: a king—and taxes. And an army. And wars to give the army an excuse for being around and spending tax money. 'I don't know,' he said, 'whether civilization *needs* slaves or *makes* slaves. It doesn't make any difference, because the fact is that civilization *has* slaves; that is what the people want, so that is what they get.'

I said, 'You can't say these kids are slaves.'

And he said: 'They live in tar paper shacks on land that produces forty-five bushels of corn per acre in a good year, and somebody in a television studio in New York tells them that the worst thing in the world is bad breath. Just use the right mouthwash and you're free from worry.'

'That don't make them slaves,' I said.

'And it doesn't make them free, either,' he said. 'But that's the trouble, Tony,' he said to me, 'there just don't seem to be any free people. Just slaves who starve. And the fat people who try to keep the slaves happy and forgetful. And maybe the fat people are more slaves than the others.'

I told him it wasn't all as simple as that. And he agreed with me again. But then he said, 'As soon as you start making things complicated, Tony, you realize that it's almost impossible even to know what the right thing is, much less to do it. And so all the goodness gets trapped inside you. "How can a man be born again?" old Nicodemus asked Jesus. And Jesus, he didn't say how; he just said to let it happen.

'And you remember Nicodemus thought he was a very grand person. "I have been a slave to no man," he said. Well, somebody said it: I am nobody's slave. And Jesus said that if you didn't know the truth you were a slave.'

And I said to him, 'There are lots of truths.'

And all Jesse said was ' "Greater love has no man except he lay down his life for. . . ." ' Now that's funny, I don't remember what the last word was: maybe it was 'friend' or 'sheep' or 'enemy.' Something like that.

—Look, Tony, the tape is only so long. You've got to stick to the subject.

—Well, I thought you wanted to know the whole story.

—But not every conversation you had with the man. Just tell me about what happened on and around March 6, 1962.

—It didn't happen out of a clear blue sky. Jesse had quite a lot of Indians stop over with him, and before long he started going to the library in town and reading about Indian history. You know, once the Sioux owned all the land in South Dakota from the Missouri River to the western boundary. And then gold was dug out of the Black Hills, and so in short order some sharp whites whittled down the size of the reservations until all the Sioux had was range land that nobody else wanted. And it was all nice and legal; it went right through Congress, and I suppose a lot of people thought we were being generous with the savage redskin.

—Get to the point, Tony.

—Well, the point is that Jesse read this sort of thing, and some nights we'd talk about it. That was in the summer of '60, and we'd sit down by the lake. It all sounds peaceful enough, except that he could never sit still very long before he was pacing along the beach. 'What do you know, Tony,' he'd ask me, 'what do you know about people who are desperate?'

'I was desperate once,' I said. 'So I ran away.' That was in Detroit, and I don't talk much about it, but I was in a bit of trouble—meaning that I was worried about getting shot through the head, from the back, all because I got mixed up in a numbers racket and didn't always take every cent out of my pocket after I'd made my collections. Of course I ran.

And Jesse asked, 'What if you couldn't run?'

'I suppose I'd fight,' I said.

'Even if you knew there wasn't any use in fighting?'
And I said, 'I don't know.'

'Have you ever been on the Twin Pine Reservation?'
he'd ask. A few times I've been through it, going to the
White River to fish. 'Were you ever by the place they call
Wounded Knee?' he'd ask. And I knew, after the first
time, pretty much what he was going to say. I don't think
it was that he'd forgotten he'd already told me the story
so much as it was that he was trying to puzzle out whatever
sense there was in it—if there was any sense in it at all. I
think that he wanted to find some point that he could
hand back to those Indian kids, maybe to give them some
kind of new picture of themselves. Anyway, it was at
Wounded Knee that the Sioux made their last big fight
against the U.S. Army. And they were massacred, men and
women and children.

That was back around 1890, when the Sioux were more
or less taken up with a man named Wovoka, a Paiute
from Nevada. This Wovoka was a strange fellow, a kind
of religious prophet, or maybe even more than a prophet.
He had this strange ghost dance that got the Indians all
stirred up. It went on for hours, and there'd be dancers
passing out and having visions and seeing their parents
who'd died five, ten years before—it was like dying for a
little while and looking into the future, or maybe even
living in it. And the way Wovoka painted it, the future
looked pretty bright for the Indians. But in the meantime,
while they was waiting for this bright future, Wovoka said
the Indians should behave themselves and put away their
guns and knives and live in peace and do right by everybody. Jesse used to say that even if the churches might not
like everything he had to say, still he seemed to have something of the spirit of Jesus about him.

And there was Sioux who traveled clear out to the West to listen to him and find out what sort of a man he was. And he told them like he told everybody else that the future depended a whole lot on whether or not they really tried to love . . . well, to love their enemies, even. Wovoka must have made some sense, because when they got back to Twin Pine they started up those ghost dances on their own. But the trouble was that they had their backs to the wall. It was like Jesse read about this one old Indian who said that the white man made a good many promises, but he really only kept one: he said he would take all of the Indian's land, and he sure enough did. And then the white man told the Indian to farm what was left; only the land was poor and the rainfall was less than poor. And the government, which promised to provide food, turned around and cut the food allowance.

And on top of that the army kept shoving and shoving these Indians onto smaller and smaller pieces of territory, kept telling them where they had to live and where they could travel and where they couldn't, and kept trying to take their guns away from them, even though these Sioux had always been raised to believe that a man couldn't be a man unless he had a gun and a horse and the freedom to ride out and shoot down his food. I mean, you've just got to wonder what kind of justice it is when one group of people tells another: From now on you've got to live and you've got to be a man the way we tell you to live and be a man, because we've got more soldiers and our guns fire more bullets than yours do.

But it seems that's pretty much the way it was. Finally there was this little band of Miniconjou Sioux under Chief Big Foot, and they was being hustled into the Twin Pine Reservation toward the end of 1890. And the U.S. Cavalry asked them to give up their guns. I guess Big Foot himself was not anxious for a fight, but some of the younger braves were not going to let themselves be pushed around by the white man. They had been involved in the ghost dances, and they probably were convinced that the future belonged to the Indian. Anyway, some of them started to fight back, and they shot a number of the troopers. And that was the beginning of the end.

Naturally, the cavalry didn't have too much choice. They had to shoot back. When the shooting was over, there were almost a hundred and fifty dead Indians. And a big hole was dug several days later, and they was thrown into it. Then the gravediggers had their picture taken, and they filled up the hole and rode back to town. 'It should not be so easy,' Jesse used to say, 'it should not be so easy for the victors to dispose of their victims.' He used to say that everybody who had power should also have an uneasy conscience.

Of course, after Wounded Knee, the Sioux were pretty well emptied out; they were licked and they knew it. That was some seventy years ago. I guess seventy years is not a long time so far as history goes; still, it is a long time to . . . well, to wait. They sit, maybe three, four thousand of them, on the Twin Pine Reservation. It's as if they was waiting for that mass grave by Wounded Knee to burst open and send out some brand-new warriors to teach them a new dream. And then there's the rest of us, us white men, who look over our shoulder every once in a while, and we act surprised that those Sioux are still sitting where we put them seventy years ago. We can fly almost up to the moon, but it don't seem that we can either show them Sioux a new way to be men or accept their old way. But maybe that's why we fly toward the moon, so we don't have to look at places like Twin Pine or ask ourselves if *we* know how to be men—without guns, that is.

That's what we talked about, me and Jesse. A white man and a Negro talking about Indians: kids like Billy White Bear and Hector Porcupine and John Caloux and Marvin Rain Cloud. They'd all heard about Big Foot and what happened at Wounded Knee, although none of them seemed to know much about the ghost dance. They were not angry kids, they were mostly sad. And they asked Jesse if he really wanted to live in a white man's world. Jesse told them that as far as he knew it wasn't a white man's world; it was God's. And they said somebody ought to tell that to the white man. And then they would laugh, softly, as though they thought it was funny but not quite humorous. They never said God, they said Wakantaka—he was the god of their fathers. They didn't want the white man's god; they were looking for Wakantaka.

'He is as near to you as your own breath,' Jesse told them. 'And you have breath. It comes to you, like a gift, without your thinking about it. But if you ever tried to chase your breath, you know you would never catch it.'

Once one of them said, 'Yes, but he must be more than breath.'

And another one said, 'Because all the white man does with him is use him to tell lies.'

'Yes,' said Jesse. 'He is also the wind that brings clouds full of rain to fall on the graves and settle them. And he is the earthquake that will open them up again.'

'That is no help to us,' the first one said.

'What you really need, then,' Jesse said, 'is someone to set you free.'

They nodded. 'But whenever God tries to do that,' Jesse said, 'there are men who try to kill him; they say he is meddling in matters that aren't his business.' Now I don't know if I've got the rest of this right, but I think that Jesse used to say something like this: that God's business is freedom, but nobody can realize that until he puts his own breathing in second place . . . and is even willing to give up breathing.

The second boy said that was too hard.

'Yes,' Jesse said. 'Except for Jesus. He cared about freedom; he let God care about his breathing.'

. Then the first boy said, 'I don't know about this Jesus. He belongs to the white man.'

'They either want him to be all theirs or they don't want him at all,' Jesse said. 'Maybe that is because people in general are more interested in capturing things than in being set free themselves. And that is your trouble, too; you don't want to live in a white man's world, but you wish that you and he might live in an Indian world.'

So that is about the way things went between 1955 and 1962. I mean, with Jesse and the Indians who visited him. There were other things that happened too, besides the Indians. Actually Jesse spent most of the time farming and helping me, especially in the winter, when we fixed up the boats and the cabins. It was the winter of '61, you remember, when my wife's sister Dorothy Mae was released from the state mental hospital in Hallmark for a trial visit, probably more because they was too crowded than because anybody thought she'd improved. Dorothy Mae's trouble isn't that she's crazy, but that she's a slow learner, and to make matters worse she was in a bad car accident once, and her nose was pushed way to one side and her jaw was broken, and it was never set right, so that it sort of hangs open.

After about three weeks in our house, what with my

wife constantly nagging her for being so slow, she was so confused it looked like we would have to send her back to the hospital. But Jesse said she could come to his house and work for him. So she went to Jesse's. And one day I was at Thorsted's for some nails and Thorsted said I was lower than a snake and smelled worse than a skunk for letting my sister work for that colored man, plus whatever else . . . 'You don't need much imagination,' he said.

But it wasn't so bad for me as it was for Jesse, because most of the stores in town stopped selling to him and he had to drive to Bankton in my pickup to get whatever he needed bad.

—But at this point, Tony, why did you stick with him? You knew he wasn't helping you any.

—I thought about it plenty, that's for sure. But the fact is that he was helping Dorothy Mae. And if there was some way to keep her out of the insane asylum, it would simply not be right to send her back. Part of her trouble was being scared most of the time. I suppose she had a reason to be, since an awful lot of people took advantage of her, one way or another. But Jesse treated her like a human being; I mean, like a lady. Oh, she worked when she was with him; but he always thanked her. And at night he'd sit and talk to her; he'd ask her what she thought about things and what she wanted out of life.

At any rate, like I said, even if Jesse was helping Dorothy Mae, he wasn't doing his reputation any good. For that matter, he wasn't doing my reputation any good. But like I said, there are some times when you have got to do things because they are right, and to hell with reputation. And I knew it was right to be a friend to Jesse Christian. Besides, I never worry about starving, not so long as I can fish and trap and hunt. And even if I did lose a few customers, it was never a matter of falling from rich to poor, but only getting a little bit poorer. And once you're poor the first time, twice as poor is not exactly a shock.

—And then March 6, 1962.

—I wondered when you was going to get around to that again. Well, the boy's name was Jack Red Elk. And he was nineteen or twenty. Jesse had never had anyone that old visit him before. And it was not just a sociable call, either. He sneaked into Jesse's house in the middle of the night, and when Jesse got up in the morning there he was, sound asleep on the kitchen floor. And his clothes was muddy and torn, like he had run across country in the dark, making sure that no one would see him. Jesse fed him, and while he was eating he didn't give any more information than his name. And when breakfast was over he fell asleep again, right in the kitchen chair. Jesse carried him into the bedroom and he didn't wake up until after dark. He found me and Jesse down by the lake, wondering when the ice would break up. He stood with us for a while, not saying anything, and finally he asked us if we were going to call the police.

Jesse said No, we didn't have any reason to, did we? And the boy said No, he didn't think so. 'Well,' said Jesse, 'maybe there are some others who do think so.'

The story came out on the way back to Jesse's house. Jack Red Elk worked on his uncle's ranch. He was trying to save enough money to go to Chicago, because that's where his girl friend had moved. He had about one hundred and fifty in the bank, and he decided to get himself a new suit, only he hated to disturb the money that was earning interest, so he went to a place where he could charge. And the man was real friendly; he said to go ahead and pick out whatever he wanted. So Jack got a suit and a topcoat, and the man in the store brought out a blank check and asked Jack to sign it. Jack said it was not from his bank, and besides Jack did not have a checking account. The man said that was all right; all he wanted was Jack's signature, and he could as well put it on this piece of paper as any other. So Jack did what the man asked. And then the man said maybe Jack would like to work off the debt instead of paying cash—he could do some painting and cleaning up around the store. And Jack agreed to this, too.

The suit was forty dollars and the topcoat was thirty-five. Jack figured that meant seventy-five hours of work, so, in the next six weeks, that's what he gave the man. But the man said that was not nearly enough. All right, Jack said that was all he was going to get, whether he liked it or not. Jack said the man just smiled and said, 'We'll see about that.'

He took the check Jack signed, and he filled it out and deposited it in his bank, and of course the check bounced. So the man took the check to the sheriff and demanded that the sheriff pick up Jack. Then he waved the check in Jack's face, and he said, 'All right, you're going to work for me until I say stop, and if you don't like that arrangement I'll have the law pick you up for passing bad checks.'

The sheriff just stood there and nodded his head; he looked at the check, and he looked at Jack, and he said to Jack, 'You're a lucky boy; this man could prefer charges, and then you'd be in for it for sure.'

That's when Jack ran away. He said that he couldn't just go to Chicago because he still had his money in the bank, and he was afraid to go back to Twin Pine to pick up his money because the sheriff was probably waiting for him and would arrest him if he showed up there.

'I don't know what to tell you,' Jesse said. 'But I guess the best thing for now is to sit tight and give yourself a few days to think things out.' The boy thought that sounded right, so he stayed . . . I guess it was almost a week that he was there. He had his days and nights mixed up: he wouldn't really wake up until suppertime, and then he prowled around, especially down by the beach—I guess it was all night long he walked by the lake, just pacing and pacing and never getting anywhere.

'Maybe I should go to Twin Pine and have a talk with that sheriff,' Jesse said to me one morning. I said that I didn't think it would do any good. No sheriff is apt to believe a stranger saying one thing when a registered voter in his own county says something else. 'Then I should talk to the store owner,' he said. But I said that if the man would pull a trick like he did to Jack, the only thing he would listen to was a stick of dynamite in his ear. Then Jesse said, 'We will just have to get together the money to send him to Chicago.' I thought that was the craziest solution yet, but finally I agreed to put in twenty-five dollars, provided that Jesse never mentioned it to my wife. And so we went into town to draw out the cash.

When we got back the boy was gone. And you know the rest of it. He'd gone over to the corral where Howard Willson keeps three, four horses for the people who stay at his place. And Jack took one of the horses and he just cut loose, yipping and bellering like a crazy man. I don't suppose that horse ever got rode so wild and so fast ever before in his life. Jack lifted him over the fence—Ralph Clinton saw it all, and he said it was a beautiful sight to behold: it looked like Jack had been riding all his life. Well, I suppose he had been, but mostly in his dreams.

Anyway, he went over the fence and down that gravel road that runs north from Willson's and past Andrew Swenson's farm. Andrew had about eighty head of beef cattle in his pasture, and Jack went over another fence and landed right in the middle of them. But by this time Ralph Clinton had called Howard Willson and said there was a horse stolen. This was all Howard Willson needed to hear; he grabbed a deer rifle and jumped into his jeep, and he was gone.

It only took a minute or so for him to drive alongside Swenson's pasture, and there was Jack, cutting that herd one way, then the other, and there was Swenson, trying to climb over the barbed-wire fence, but he was caught on the barbs, and he was screaming for somebody to do something. Well, Howard Willson did something: he fired a shot in the air. Jack reined his horse up short and headed for the road—over the fence and right for Willson's jeep. Willson shot once more; the horse fell right from under Jack, and he rolled into the ditch.

Now we was on the scene too, me and Jesse, in my pickup, maybe a hundred yards behind Willson. And we saw Jack come out of the ditch. He looked around, kind of shaky, until he spotted Willson. He straightened himself out, and he walked nice and calm and steady toward Willson. And then, just as nice and easy, Howard Willson raised that rifle and fired one shot through the boy's forehead. And Jack was dead.

After that he laid his gun beside him and turned the jeep around and drove home. He never looked right or left; he pretended not to notice us, and maybe he didn't.

It was pretty plain to see that the boy was beyond help. But Jesse just kneeled down in the road and held Jack's head in his lap. That's the way it was when the sheriff got there, with Andrew Swenson beside him. 'Howard Willson did it,' Jesse said. 'The boy was unarmed and Willson shot him.' The sheriff didn't say a word; he looked at Jesse like Jesse was dirt and the boy was not even as good as dirt; then he motioned to Swenson, and the two of them lifted Jack's body and threw him into the trunk of the sheriff's car.

Afterward the sheriff said that the county only paid him mileage, it did not provide a car, so he had to drive his own, and he did not want to get the uphostery dirty, and he figured it didn't make any difference since the boy was dead anyway.

We followed the sheriff into town and we took the boy and laid him out. We took him back to Twin Pine, too. Nobody there seemed much concerned. Both his parents were dead; they died of tuberculosis before the boy was twelve years old. His uncle more or less tried to raise him, but he already had nine kids, so he never went much out of his way to help Jack. 'It ain't that I'm not sorry to hear it,' he said. 'But there ain't nothing I can do about it now.' He turned away from me then, and he spoke to Jesse: 'The one good thing about a reservation,' he said, 'you don't have to mess with the white man.' Jesse tried to convince him that something should be done, because Jack had been murdered. We were in the uncle's home, a big log house that smelled of grease and wood smoke. There wasn't any electricity in the house and they still used an outhouse ten yards behind the house. 'You know Jack wrote a bad check,' the uncle said. 'And if I get things stirred up, if I demand my justice, the man from the store will probably bring the sheriff out here and make me pay off the check. And that might just make me so damn mad I would kill the both of them.' He got up and went to the door and pointed toward a small grove of trees to the southeast. 'Jack used to like that place. If you want to do me a favor, you can bury him there.'

And so we did, me and Jesse. We found two shovels back of the house, and we carried the boy to the grove, and we dug a grave for him. Jesse found a saw and a hammer and some nails by the barn, and he made a cross and scratched the boy's name on the cross. When we was finished and the cross was up, we stood for a minute without saying anything; finally Jesse said, 'In the name of the Father, Son, and Holy Ghost. Amen.' And we drove back to Nortonville.

The next week, Jesse went to see the county attorney, a man named Albertson. Albertson is a young man, and he is ambitious. That pretty well sums it up. Anyway, you know that he is running for the U.S. Senate now, and Howard Willson is right up there telling everybody what a fine man he is and running ads in the newspapers for him. Well, Albertson is a fine man, and I would not be surprised if I voted for him. He is all for helping the poor and the old, and since I am already poor and I am not getting any younger, it is only the smart thing to do. Just the same, in March of 1962 Jesse went to see him, and Albertson said that of course there would be a trial during the fall term of court, but there was not much evidence to go on. Jesse said that there might be some question, but it was open-and-shut manslaughter because Jack Red Elk had no weapon and he wasn't even running, he was walking toward Willson.

'Swenson said he was running,' Albertson said.

Jesse told him that we were as close as Swenson.

But Albertson reminded him that we were behind Willson. And we were. And not only that, Albertson said, but

Willson was after a horse thief, and he was performing a citizen's arrest.

But he never said anything to the boy. He never said, 'Hands up,' or 'Stop,' or anything. Albertson said that was because he was excited. The question was not whether or not Willson was guilty, Albertson said, but whether the killing was justified. Albertson said that he would do what he could, but, after all, the boy was in trouble with the law back home too, and if he hadn't been shot he would have been in trouble here. And, speaking of Willson, he said that you don't like to ruin a man's life because he made one mistake.

The next day, Albertson saw me on the street, and he said, 'It's too bad this had to happen.' I said Yes, it was. 'And between the two of us,' he said, 'I do not have much sympathy for Howard Willson. I would like to go after him.' So I said that's just what he should do. 'That would make three of us,' he said. 'You and me and that Christian fellow. And the two of you couldn't care less what people think. But the people in this town are my bread and butter. And last year Howard Willson paid me eight hundred dollars in fees. Oh, I could stand to lose that. I'm not entirely money-hungry. But if I go after Howard Willson, the chances are that I won't be able to get him, and the people around here will say—well, they won't say that I'm doing it in the interest of justice. They will say that I am a Negro and Indian lover, and that if I love them so much maybe I should go to work for them and let them support me. No, sir,' he said. 'You and your friend, you go to the churches, and you tell the ministers to work on the people, tell them to get their people worked up about justice, and then maybe I'll have the guts to operate according to justice, too.'

When I told Jesse what Albertson had said, he shook his head. 'No,' he said, 'it would never work. The churches are too interested in building new buildings and keeping people happy.'

'But what else can you do?' I asked him.

'All right,' he said, after a long pause. 'I'll try it.'

On Sunday we went to Reverend Goodwin's church; Jesse asked me along so that I could pray. 'For you,' I said.

'For everybody,' he said. 'Especially for the Holy Spirit.'

I said that I would do what I could, but I didn't know the words too good.

'Just say, "Come, Holy Spirit," ' he said.

We were a few minutes late, so we sat at the back. The ushers looked surprised, but they didn't do anything. They just kept their eyes on us, like we was bank robbers or something.

I suppose the service was the same as usual; there were hymns and prayers and readings from the Bible and announcements and a sermon. Goodwin seems to be a pretty good preacher. He talked about how Jesus had to go up to Jerusalem in the end because that's where all the power was, and so if what he had to say was going to make any dent on the people it had to reach the leaders there as well as the poor people in Galilee. And then, he said, Jesus found out that the place where he got the poorest reception was in the Temple, the religious headquarters. So he threw out the moneylenders or whoever they were on the Temple porch, not just because they were crooks, but because he was frustrated that nobody would listen to him, that they didn't want to hear the truth.

It was an interesting sermon, and I was listening, so I didn't even hear or see Jesse get up, but when the sermon was over there he was, standing in the aisle. The ushers were standing right in back of him, holding the collection plates and looking at one another, each one, I guess, wishing that the next one would do something. But they just stood there. And Jesse walked down the aisle until he was right by the pulpit. And Reverend Goodwin just stared at him; his mouth was open, but it seemed that he couldn't find a single word to say. The rest of the people looked at one another. I saw Howard Willson sitting toward the front; he turned around, and I swear he looked positively scared.

'I apologize for being here today,' Jesse started out. His voice trembled, and he cleared his throat. When he spoke again his voice was stronger. 'No,' he said, 'I do not apologize for being in the house of God or speaking in the house of God, because I want you to look at something.' He went to the ushers and he took the plates from them, and they didn't say or do anything this time, either. Maybe they thought it was something that Goodwin and Jesse had planned between them. But Goodwin looked awfully uncomfortable; he hadn't made a move since Jesse got up.

Jesse held the plates up high. 'What is this?' he asked. 'Do you think you can pay God once a week to keep his eyes off you? Do you think that's all he expects from you?' He let the plates drop on the floor. They was brass or copper, I don't know, but they rolled down the aisle and finally clattered to a rest like two spinning silver dollars. Then Jesse spotted Howard Willson, and he looked right at him and said, 'Blood money.'

By then I was edging toward the door. I was the only one who was moving, and I was in the vestibule when Jesse started up the aisle again. The ushers stepped aside for him like the Red Sea for Moses. We just stepped outside and a rumbling began in the church—feet scraping and people talking in loud whispers. Howard Willson was the next one out the door after us. Jesse never looked back, but I did. And I saw Willson pointing his finger at us. 'We'll see who has the last word,' he said.

Jesse just kept walking. He didn't say anything until we were in my pickup. Then he said, 'Well, did you remember to pray?'

'No,' I said, 'I forgot. Things happened too fast.'

'You aren't happy about what happened, are you?' he asked me.

I didn't know how to answer him. I guess that what I really wanted to see happen was . . . to have Howard Willson destroyed. But I knew that was not what Jesse wanted. Actually, I didn't know what Jesse wanted. Finally I said, 'No, I am not happy.'

'I am sick unto death,' he said. And the rest of the way home we rode in silence.

—And that's it?

—What else do you want?

—Do you think he knew what was going to happen? Do you think Howard Willson scared him?

—No, I don't think he knew *what* exactly would come. But he was ready.

—Wasn't there some other way?

—There were lots of other ways. He could have kept quiet. But I think he felt he had kept quiet long enough. It was sort of like going up to Jerusalem, if you know what I mean.

December 23, 1962

Dear Lee,

This isn't the Christmas card I planned to send. The first one I picked was funny: Santa Claus was landing his sleigh at the North Pole, and there was one package left in back; a beautiful girl was wriggling out of the package and Santa was looking at her, leering. The girl was saying, "See what Santa forgot," and then, on the inside, "But I still love you a lot."

I thought it was cute, so I bought it, almost a month ago. Then I started debating whether or not I should send it —I wasn't sure exactly what the implications were. For either of us. I mean, it's been a long time. And maybe it would be better to send something that didn't have any implications at all, or else was completely obvious.

But yesterday I saw this card, and I didn't hesitate. Just the baby Jesus, all by himself in the middle of a desert. "Peace on earth to men of good will." Somehow that makes a lot more sense than the other way: "Good will to men."

Mother and Daddy are here with me. As usual. Our third Christmas away from Nortonville; our third Christmas without snow. I'm quite used to it. I have my own apartment this year, and there's a big Christmas tree that takes up the whole living room. We went into the mountains a few days ago and spent seven dollars for the privilege of cutting it down ourselves. It's funny, but when Daddy is here I seem to get very conscious about the price of things. Last night our dinner cost $9.35, plus tip. Daddy hates to tip—I think he left only fifty cents. So I try to steer him away from the places where I normally eat.

Tonight, though, just the two of us went out. Mother wasn't feeling well, just a cold, I guess. We went to a place that Mother would very definitely have frowned upon, a Mexican restaurant where we had tacos and enchiladas and a dark brown, thick, kind of sweet Mexican beer. And there was sawdust on the floor and, honest, the waiters licked their fingers. It wasn't very Christmasy, and I didn't think Daddy would like it very much. But the prices were low; he liked that. And after Christmas shopping with Mother for the past three days, about eight hours a day, he was ready for something un-Christmasy and masculine, which this place was, what with the sawdust and the tables that smelled like they'd been soaked for ten years in sweat and beer.

It's called Pedro's, and it's a college hangout. But since almost everybody is home, the place was only half filled and very quiet. Even so, the service was terribly slow; for over half an hour we didn't have anything to do but sit and sip beer and talk. That's something we'd really never done before, not just sip beer, but talk. Part of the time we talked about you—the first time we'd mentioned your name in each other's presence since I left Nortonville.

First Daddy said that Jesse Christian had been killed, hit by a car while he was walking up the lake road one night. And then I asked Daddy if he was the one that had Jesse beat up. Just like that. Daddy seemed surprised, not that I'd suspect him, but that I hadn't known all along.

Maybe I had known—why else would I have asked him?

But I didn't know, honest, that you were mixed up in it. I asked him who did the job for him, and when he said your name, all of a sudden I wanted to be completely left alone.

That was the moment when at last I stopped pretending that it was at least partially your idea that I not have the baby. I take that mistake, or guilt, or sin, or whatever you want to call it, all to myself. Because it was my idea, entirely. I thought there would be nothing to it, except maybe a few miserable days, like a bad case of flu. And neither one of us would be hurt. "Surprise, surprise!" says Old Lady Justice. "I have something else in store for you." The more authority you take for disposing your deeds, the more you realize how weak your authority really is. I meant to set us free—and look what I caused. Maybe I ought to pray. But I'm not sure for what.

Anyway, I did this much: I told Daddy that it was all my own fault.

And Daddy blustered and blushed. "Well," he said, "you didn't seduce him, did you?" No, I didn't, but it was mutual, wasn't it?

And our not getting married was mutual too—that's what I told Daddy. I was willing to, but I never insisted. "What it would amount to," you said, "is taking the medicine that tastes the best. And that's not the same as taking the best medicine." I agreed, even though I wasn't sure—and still am not—what that best medicine is. Just the same, I could have fought; I could have been very tenacious and clung to you. In so many words, that's what I told Daddy: that I hadn't been willing to be your puppy and that I had never wanted his money or my condition to buy me a good home and respectability.

So I took care of my condition. "And that should have put a stop to the story," I said to Daddy. Because he didn't have to get you involved in it, or Jesse Christian. Not at that point. Because he didn't help, he couldn't help to change things.

Daddy said that was right, he knew all the time that neither money nor violence would make any difference. And he found out too late that Jesse Christian had nothing to do with my . . . "Abortion," I said. He blushed again; it was both funny and sad: poor strong Daddy and his poor barren daughter who learned too much before her time, but too late for it to do any good.

After that word—my second scarlet letter, you might say—we sat and looked into our beer, until Daddy finally said, "I had to do something." So naturally he went to you, and naturally he figured that Jesse Christian was wrapped into the deal because you had stayed with him. And it was sheer, simple justice to put you both into the same pen to chew each other up: Jesse the devil and you his protégé.

Only you knew better than that, Lee. My poor blind, bullheaded father thought he was serving justice, but you knew that it was not justice to attack Jesse Christian. You knew, and all you had to do was tell my father that Jesse Christian had nothing to do with my being in the hospital —but you didn't. Were you afraid that if you didn't play the part of the middleman you'd have to take that of the low man? Did you think it was a choice between hitting or getting hit?

I asked my father what he thought. I told him tonight, Lee, that you had known all the time that you were beating an innocent man. And Daddy wasn't shocked at all. Abortion can shock him, but not that kind of brutality—

it's curious, isn't it, that men should have a much harder
time than women accepting the functions and malfunctions
of the body? Maybe that's why it's easier for a man to be
indecently brutal to another man's body: it's only a piece
of machinery, with parts. I hate that phrase, "parts of the
body." But I suppose you thought that as long as you
were only hurting a part of his body and not killing the
whole body, it wasn't really such a terrible thing to do.

And then, too, you got paid for it. Daddy said it wasn't
just for giving Jesse the beating. He thinks he could have
forced you into that without paying for it. No, the money
is part of his idea of justice—the money you've been getting every month since you went to college. You probably
thought it was a straight business transaction, but Daddy
has this primitive idea that whenever you overpay a man
you obligate him. So you took and took, and you're still
taking from Daddy—but, Lee, it isn't just to cover up the
man behind Jesse Christian's beating. Daddy isn't that
afraid of being found out; he suspects that everyone in
town knows the truth anyway. No, you're getting paid to
remember, to remember what you did to me and what
you did to Jesse and what you forced Daddy to do.

I'm not talking now about my getting pregnant. That
was mutual. But then getting married was simply not the
"best medicine." And you lived with Jesse Christian. Later
on you beat him up, and after that you took Daddy's
money and probably pretended you were doing him a
favor. I mean, every time you ought to have taken a stand
you sidestepped; you wanted to be on everybody's side,
mine and Jesse's and Daddy's. You could have married me,
you could have stayed at Jesse's, you could have said No
to Daddy, you could have thrown Daddy's money in his
face. But instead you skimmed by.

Tonight I told Daddy to stop sending you money. He said he wasn't through with you yet, but I asked him to let you go. "Don't you want something more from him?" he asked me slowly.

"Jesse Christian's dead," I said. "The book is closed." I mean, I'm willing to put all the damage that all of us did into the grave with him, and start over again with a clean slate. You know, Lee, guilt is a vicious thing—it started with just the two of us doing a very private, very happy thing, and then I did a foolish thing and you did a brutal thing, and maybe his death can be traced directly back to us. Well, we can't keep paying forever—I guess that's all I mean, that we've got to turn in our bad will, we've got to stop living on the basis of that bad investment we made almost three years ago. I mean, everything worked up to his death, and now it's all over, and we can make a new beginning.

That's why the checks aren't going to be in the mail every month. No strings attached anymore. Daddy asked if I ever heard from you, or ever wrote. I said I was innocent on both counts. So Daddy said he would close the books, write it off—at first he said it would be like a bad debt, but I said No to that; it was an investment.

"No," he said. "Payment for services rendered. But now he's on his own."

I must hurry along now, since it's almost two in the morning, and I know tomorrow will be busy with wrapping presents—and guess what? I'm going to fix the Christmas Eve dinner all by myself: turkey and dressing and cranberry sauce and sweet potatoes and all the other usual things—and me, the Grand Hostess!

Lee, why don't you come, too? Or let me come to you. We could start all over again; we never got a fair chance the last time, too many people got in our way. But there wouldn't be any strings attached this time. I'd be willing to work to put you through school. We could go where-ever you wanted to.

It's almost three now, and for the past half hour I've been rereading and rereading the paragraph above. It isn't as well written as I'd like, but I'll stand by it just the same. And I'll stand by everything that went before it, because it's all true, including the unflattering things I have to say about you. I know that you could find someone else easily enough, and simply forget what happened between us and around us. But that would be the worst sin of all—to pretend you're another pleasant, normal American boy, when the fact is that you, both of us, descended into hell. And now we're out of it again, and we've paid all there is to pay, and we know all there is to know—and we don't have to blame each other any more, we can simply and blessedly accept each other because we've got the founda-tion for it: we've been forgiven—given up for dead and then given over for life.

I don't dare go any further. I don't know what else to say, except that I want you back again. Such as I am, I want you. No illusions left. But still some passion. For you.

My love,
Marie

January 1, 1963

Dear Marie,

I don't know exactly how to begin. Maybe the best way is to tell you what happened when my father and I went to see Jesse. There have never been more than three who knew, and now that Jesse's gone there are only two, so you can be the one who fills out the circle.

First of all, your father talked to both of us, my father and me. And he never mentioned violence; he only said something about setting the record straight. And he left us to draw our own conclusions. But you're right about one thing: I said absolutely nothing in Jesse's behalf, said nothing about his innocence. I went along; I said nothing to your father, and I followed my father. The only promise we got was that we'd be taken care of. But I didn't have the slightest idea what that meant, except that I thought it might work both ways—we'd be taken care of if we went, but also if we didn't go. I know I shouldn't have just gone along like that. My father had been drinking, and I knew something bad might happen, but I was scared. Here was a chance for me to get off the hook and put together all those dreams of mine that we used to talk about, dreams that were lying in broken pieces at my feet. Not very noble, was it?

Well, anyway, we went—and for my father "setting the record straight" meant only one thing: teaching Jesse once and for all that he wasn't wanted, that he didn't belong in our town. This was going to be accomplished, according to my father, by "pounding a little sense into his head." And I went along, saying nothing.

When we got to Jesse's, he let us in; he seemed glad to see us. He'd never met my father. He offered his hand, and my father took it. My father actually seemed friendly— because he was going to try to get some money from Jesse. He explained that I was in an obviously embarrassing situation and that I couldn't expect much sympathy from anybody in town, so maybe Jesse, who had proven his loyalty by taking me in, might want to help my cause by getting up enough money to pay my way out of town. I sat there and said nothing—I had expected this least of all. Not that I expected violence, either—just a bit of drunken growling (because my father had been drinking) and table-pounding.

But instead he begged. Jesse was reluctant. He asked me if I still planned to go to college, and in a whisper I said, "Someday, I hope." He told me I should start right away, and then my father whimpered that he'd lost his job and couldn't provide any help. I had a little bit saved, you know, and I had a small scholarship, but I needed that little extra boost from my father. So it did look pretty hopeless for me and my future—no place to go but away, or else to Jesse's. And here was my father, destroying that refuge. And I just sat there, while my father wheedled and begged for my getaway money as though I were some sort of thief fleeing in the night.

Finally, Jesse asked, "If I helped you, would you go to school?"

Before I had a chance to answer, my father said that I certainly would, and I'd appreciate it an awful lot. My father oozed a sickening sincerity, and I hated him as I have never hated anyone before or since, hated him particularly because he was exhibiting my blood, the soil in which I was (like it or not) rooted.

So Jesse got up and went to his cupboard and reached in—and my father took a catsup bottle that was on the table and clubbed Jesse with it, clubbed him twice. And Jesse fell to the floor. I can remember my mouth opening, but I can't remember any sound coming out. I sat and watched. My father went into the yard and brought back a chain, and he started to beat Jesse with it. He swung down and let the chain slash through his clothes . . . and after each slashing he leaned over to feel Jesse's pulse. And when he was satisfied the pulse was still strong, he slashed him again. To nobody in particular he said, "I want to make it look authentic," as though he were preparing the set for a play. I'd never heard my father use a word that big before—"authentic." I suppose he'd heard it on television and was trying to impress me that he knew what he was doing: slash and then listen for life, as methodical as a man on an assembly line doing his job. Perhaps if it had been a furious violence I might have intervened, drawn in by the excitement and tension. But it was utterly calm, almost peaceful, except for the rattling of the chain.

Finally my father decided that Jesse had had enough. The chain was bloody, and some of the blood was on my father's hands and clothing. He dropped the chain across Jesse's body and went to the cupboard. Soon he brought out the little bowl that Jesse had been reaching for, a bowl stuffed with bills. My father sat down across the table from me and counted, mostly ones and fives, adding up to nearly three hundred dollars. He announced the sum, as proud as though he'd earned it himself, by the sweat of his brow. Well, he did work for it, he was sweating. "That sure was lucky," he said, looking down at the money. "That sure was lucky."

And at last I said something: "Lucky for who?"

My father seemed surprised that I would accuse him, even mildly, of wrongdoing. "Well," he said, "I did it all for you."

"But he was going to give it to us anyway," I said.

"Well," my father said, "I was just afraid he'd hold something back on us."

And that's all there was to it, that's the story. Once my father found out he could have his old job back, he gave me the money. And that's how I got through freshman year. And the money your father sent I mailed back to my father. I suppose he drank it up, most of it.

There is one other item, a letter from Jesse. I received it a few weeks after school started. And now I'm copying it for you to read—without comment:

Dear Lee,

I am not a very practiced letter writer. But this is special. I have to write this because I do not know any other way to get in touch with you. I cannot be silent about the visit you and your father made. In the Bible Jesus talks about the Kingdom of Heaven and men coming to take it by force. Men of violence. I never understood that before. Now I do, from your visit. And I understand your visit from Jesus' words. Violence doesn't work.

Oh, in a way it does. I have something to show for it. On my back. And you have something in your pocketbook.

111

But nothing is settled. I see your father on the street, and if he sees me first he crosses the street. How can I explain it? There is no ease. Once, you and I fished and talked together. Now that's been spoiled, that little kingdom we had when we took what God gave us and shared it. What's good is given. What's taken is broken. We won't wait for the whole kingdom to come, so we attack it and break off a small part of it. It's something, but it doesn't entirely satisfy, like the taste of blood that only makes some animals want more and more. Actually, I'm surprised your father could stop before he killed me. Not out of love, I am sure, but out of fear.

As for the money, I meant to give it to you anyway, and let it rest at that. But I wanted it to be a blessing to you. And maybe it's too late for that. I hold that against you more than anything else. You cheated me of the chance to give a blessing. Now all I can give you is forgiveness. Whenever you ask for it. That's the one thing that violence can't carry away. And I guess that's really the heart of the Kingdom of Heaven and being at ease in it.

Sincerely,
Jesse

I meant to answer him. I carried the letter in my bill-fold, and, for a while, every time I opened my billfold I was reminded that *tonight* I would have to write to him. In my mind I composed hundreds of letters. But I never got a single one written. And when I learned that he was dead I was tremendously relieved. I should have thrown his letter away then. My mistake was in keeping it—the relic of a dead, silent saint. I'm above praying to relics (this one is only a piece of paper, after all), but what am I going to do? Forget about it, about him?

I suppose so. I've done a fairly good job of that already. I eat well, I lose no sleep over him, I look forward to the future with mild optimism, I believe that basically God likes me the way I am.

And now your letter. The murderer of her child writes to a thief in the night, two very pretty people sharing dark confidences. And you suggest that we belong together. We do, like Adam and Eve, or Ahab and Jezebel. And Jesse's our Elijah, whom we try to murder. But he keeps coming back, he keeps his words and our deeds alive.

And there's no more money coming every month. The kingdom I tried to take by force has at last been lifted from me. I've got no regrets. Actually, it's a kind of freedom.

So, with this freedom, I'll say what I have to say. That this is the kind of letter I wanted to write to Jesse. And yours is the kind that I hoped Jesse would send in return. In a way, then, the circle is complete. And I can turn away from the sight of myself on that kitchen chair, sitting, staring, doing nothing—even though I can't forget it. I mean, your Adam is ready. For better, for worse, with no kingdom to bring. With my father's blood, and with our Judas money all, thank God, spent. I tell you, Yes. Yes.

With love,
Lee

April 14, 1963

(From the Diary of Pfc. Paul Westfield)

I told Captain Harris this morning that my struggle with the army is over a very basic issue: I don't feel that I can work wholeheartedly for any organization whose purpose is killing. Captain Harris said that I was guilty of over-simplification.

"I've never killed anybody in my life," he said. "And I've been in the army fourteen years."

"But just the same," I said, "you must believe that conflicts can be settled by force. And force includes killing. And I don't believe that force really settles anything."

"You're naive," he said. "Maybe force doesn't settle anything. But force exists, it has arms and legs as well as a brain. And the army is simply a method, a tried and tested method for controlling and disciplining the arms and legs of force. The question is not whether to have an army, but only how to keep it both lean and disciplined so it can move fast and orderly and obediently. Killing has little or nothing to do with it. Killing is simply an accident, a kind of side effect that can happen whenever the brain of force unleashes its arms and legs. It's like holding a police dog on a leash: you keep the leash tight while you're walking by a playground, but late at night when a thug leaps out of an alley you let loose, you give the dog free rein for your protection. The power is there all the time in the dog, but the man behind the dog must decide when to utilize the power. The dog himself, brute force, is quite neutral, morally speaking."

"That made beautiful sense," I said. "But I don't like it."

"Nobody asks you to like it," the captain said. "Just obey."

We were having coffee in the basement of the church after the service. The captain and I are fellow alumni, although he was graduated from Hauge College ten years before I was. In a mild sort of way he considers himself a philosopher, but I tell him that his philosophy is essentially "Might makes right."

Naturally, he objects. He claims that I'm biased against the military, and I'm also too eager to stick people into pigeonholes—a sin which I'm afraid I am guilty of. My usual reply is that the only aggression that really changes anything is the aggression of love, which ends in sacrifice.

Sarcastically he answers: "Do you think that ought to form the basis for our national policy?"

But I pay no attention, I continue: "And the only victory is resurrection."

"I'm not prepared to argue that point," he says. "I was talking about short-range goals. I know that guns will never build a perfect peace, but as a military man I'm satisfied with imperfect peace. And under those terms I think it's preferable to demolish a city of five thousand with guns and bombs in order to prevent an atomic attack on New York—or Moscow, or Peking, for that matter."

"But I don't think that's the right choice," I say, becoming a bit more heated now. "One act of violent aggression leads to another. And each act is a little larger. The real alternative is between taking arms and laying them down. Either you're willing to kill or you're determined not to. And if you're determined not to, then you must be willing to . . . well, to lay down your life."

"You aren't willing to be a killer," he says. "But you're willing to make others into killers. That seems to be a peculiar sort of arrogance."

"Not if you accept your killer's guilt at the same time that you accept the death he gives you. And then, sooner or later, your killer will realize that the way of the killer is the way of death—he'll stop seeking out death and he'll try to reconcile himself to life."

"In theory, at least," the captain says. "But if you feel this way, what are you doing in the army?"

"I was drafted."

"And if you have to fight, if someone comes after you with a bayonet fixed on the end of his rifle, what then?"

With much sadness I answer, "I don't know."

But today is Easter, no day for sadness. Jesus Christ is risen from the dead: Alleluia!

Last Easter—April 22, Anno Domini 1962—Jesse Christian died. Several times this morning I was about to tell the captain about Jesse, but in the context of our conversation Jesse Christian didn't quite make sense—or perhaps he made more sense than we were capable of understanding. I mean, what does make sense in our sparkling and unreal age? Do Cadillacs make sense in Harlem? Do swimming pools make sense in the backyards of bankers while slum kids have to fight to get a hydrant turned on? And what sense does napalm make? (I have heard here that the smell of human flesh is not unlike the smell of roast pork—I wonder if it makes your mouth water.)

I mean, at the moment I am sick of America. And I am ashamed of myself for being sick, for assuming a kind of moral superiority, because I know very well that I am (like it or not) thoroughly and wholeheartedly American, and all the raging I do against my country is also a raging against my own impotency. For all my arguments in behalf of sacrifice, what have I ever sacrificed in the name of love? The captain, at least, is prepared to act on his faith in America's responsibility to bring peace and light to the world: he obeys. On the other hand, I doubt that my country knows anything but the most elementary facts about peace and light: the practical result of America's growth in power has been her growth in guilt, and what have I done to heal? But they who are ill, they need a physician. Physician, where art thou? Not I, not I. But he who sacrificed and died? He who rose?

He who died? Jesse Christian. Last Easter I was in Florida, in search of fun and sun. I drank too much, I got a sunburn, and on Easter Sunday I heard a preacher talk from a pickup truck: he said that Jesus was the way and the truth and the life. All I knew was that life on a Florida beach was really living, but I doubted that it was *the* life —I knew it wasn't the whole truth—and the way? Well, who does know the way? There are lots of ways.

My mother wrote to me about Jesse's outbreak in church; she said that it had been shocking. Others told me about it that summer; I judged from them that it had been more than shocking, or perhaps less than shocking: they had been insulted. Clarence Lirrpa, a good Baptist, whose son was a classmate of mine, had quite another point of view, or seemed to: "They had it coming to them," he said. "But it's too bad it had to come from him."

Tony Sauer just shook his head when I asked him about

it. It was three weeks before I was scheduled to go into the army, and I was sitting on his dock, fishing. Finally he said, "It's a nice sunset tonight." I agreed. "Sometimes," he said, "you can almost believe it's a peaceful world."

"For a few minutes, at least," I said. "If you're a forgetful man."

"I really miss that man," he said. He was fishing with a cane pole; he brought up the line and looked at the dead minnow on his hook; he looked at it for a long time, as if he couldn't decide whether to put a fresh one on or not, but at last he tossed the line, and the same minnow, back in the water. "I just have the idea that he had more to tell us, that he died too soon."

"That's true with everybody, isn't it?"

"I guess so," he said. "He had his last meal with us, you know."

"No, I didn't know that."

"What did you hear?"

"He was walking up the gravel road that leads to Martin's Landing. He was on the wrong side of the road, and it was late at night. Bill Fernley was taking that last curve before you get to the Landing, and Jesse was practically in the middle of the road. Bill couldn't stop, he hit him, and Jesse died. Right on the spot."

"Have you talked to many people about it?" Tony asked.

"Not many people want to talk about it," I said. "It's one thing to hate a man while he's still alive. But after he's dead . . . well, it's a little like grave robbing."

"Do you think people really hated him?"

"Maybe hate isn't exactly the right word," I said. "I know they didn't like him. But when he got up in church, that was apparently the last straw. I mean, it was bad enough that he wasn't like the rest of us, but when he came right out and said that he didn't want to be like us, that it wasn't good enough for him to be like us, I guess he became a kind of bone in the throat—he wouldn't come up and he wouldn't go down."

"Well, he finally went down, all the way down," Tony said.

"What really happened?"

"He was eating with us. It was Easter night; we were having a little celebration. It was Jesse's idea; he said we ought to celebrate Jesus' resurrection. You know, he was a preacher once; he traveled around in Texas, he stopped in different towns and he'd preach for three, four nights, sometimes in a church and sometimes just on a street corner. That's what he figured his real job was, preaching. Only sometimes, he said, he did his preaching with a fish pole in his hands, and the fish was his congregation. Anyway, my wife and myself and my wife's sister was there with him; he said we was his congregation that night. And we had a big pan full of bluegills and a little wine that he'd made from some wild grapes. We'd just finished up when the telephone rang; a man was talking—he sounded a little tight—and he wanted Jesse. Jesse took the phone, but he didn't say much, just Yes every few seconds.

"After he hung up, Jesse told us that it was an Indian from Twin Pine; he'd been in an accident up near Martin's Landing and he'd heard that Jesse Christian was a good man to call for help.

" 'But how would he know to call my place?' I asked Jesse. And Jesse said it was the Holy Spirit guiding him. I said I didn't believe that, and Jesse smiled and said he didn't believe it, either.

" 'Do you know what I believe?' I said. 'I believe it's

somebody that wants to start a little trouble.' And Jesse admitted that was more than possible. So I said to him that I thought he'd better stay right where he was. But no, he said he was going to walk up to Martin's Landing, because even if it wasn't an Indian who needed help, it was somebody who wanted him.

" 'Well, of course it's somebody who wants you,' I said. 'But they sure don't want you for anything good.'

" 'But I have to go to them,' he said, 'so that once and for all, whoever they are, they can get a good taste of the horror they want to sink themselves into.'

"I told him I'd take him, but he said he wanted to go alone. I told him he was crazy, and he said he probably was—a damn fool, he said.

"And then he stopped, he was right by the door, and he said, 'No, not a damn fool, not on Easter.' And then he left. As soon as he was up by the road I got ready to follow him, only my wife said there was no use in two crazy people getting hurt. And I argued with her—the truth is that I really wanted her to argue me out of going after him, because I knew he was going to get hurt and I didn't want to be with him. I let the argument drag out over half an hour, until at last my wife's sister said that if I was a friend of his I didn't have any excuse not to be with him.

" 'Just because I'm a friend of his,' I said, 'is no reason I have to be crazy, too.' She didn't say anything, but she went to the door and held it open. My wife didn't say anything this time. So I went.

"I went through the woods and then along the lake shore up to the Landing. Then I cut up to the road. When I heard voices I got down on my belly and crawled to the edge of the brush by the road. There was a car in the middle of the road, and in the headlights I could make out Dale Willson and Bremer Geare and Bill Fernley. Bremer had something in his hands, a piece of pipe or maybe a big stick. And they was all looking down at something laying in the road—it looked like a pile of old clothes, it didn't move or anything. But right away I knew it was Jesse. And I just crouched down; I wanted to sink into the ground. The last thing in my mind was to get up and do something, unless it was to vomit.

"At first I couldn't make out anything that any of them was saying; I'm pretty sure they was all drunk, even Bremer, and they was kind of laughing, pointing at Jesse and laughing. But after a while, after they had prodded him and he didn't move, they stopped laughing, and I could hear Bremer say, 'I think our fun is over, boys.'

"Bill Fernley walked over to the car, and he said, 'Well, Dale, I guess this is what your old man wanted anyway.'

" 'You keep my old man out of it,' Dale said.

"And Bremer said, 'Well, it was his idea, wasn't it, to rough him up a little?'

"And Bill said, 'We was just trying to be good Indians, is all,' and he laughed, but nobody else did.

"Dale kept saying that his old man, Howard Willson, had better be kept out of it, because he was in enough trouble as it was, and he also knew how to make trouble. Bremer never argued that point, but he said that they'd all better start thinking of some way to get out of this mess.

"Bill Fernley went over to Jesse and got down on his hands and knees and put his ear onto Jesse's chest. 'Well,' he said, 'it ain't no mess for him anymore. Of course, it could have been those Indians he was always seeing; they

121

wouldn't have hesitated over something like this, not if there was a chance of making a few dollars.'

"So Fernley rolled Jesse's body over and took out his wallet. 'I'll flip you for it,' he said, and he took out a coin from his own pocket. The other two said that was all right, so Fernley flipped the coin in the air and Dale and Bremer called it. Dale won, so he and Fernley flipped again, and this time Fernley won. He looked into the wallet and took out a few bills, and then he stuffed it back into Jesse's pocket. 'He might need it for identification, wherever he's going,' Fernley said.

" 'I got a better idea,' Bremer said. He explained how they could hold Jesse up and Fernley could take his car and come around the curve down the road and they could throw Jesse against the car. That way Fernley could bring Jesse in, and it would be reported as an accident. And there was no relatives that anybody knew about to ask for an investigation. So that's what they did: they dragged Jesse's body up the road, and Fernley backed his car up, and I crawled away. When I got back home I told my wife and her sister that I wasn't able to find Jesse."

"And you never reported what you saw?" I asked him.

"Who would've believed me?" Tony said.

"I believe you," I said. "Haven't you told anyone else?"

"Reverend Goodwin," he said. "He came down here the day after Jesse was brought in, and he said that he would like to have the funeral. I told him that was all right with me. He said he wanted to have it in the church. I said that might not be a very smart thing to do, and then I told him what I'd seen. But he said he wanted to have the funeral there anyway. I went, and so did my wife and her sister and Mrs. Goodwin. That was all. And we buried him in old Cartwright's plot. Reverend Goodwin figured that it would do Cartwright good to have some company."

"But didn't Goodwin do anything else, didn't he try to report what you'd seen?"

I didn't expect any answer, and I didn't get one. Tony took his line out of the water, pulled the minnow off the hook and threw it back into the lake, and walked to his house. "Good night," I called to him, but he kept walking.

The next day I went to see Alex Goodwin. I was angry, and in anger I prepared a violent speech: You call yourself a disciple of Christ, and yet you allow murder to occur on your very doorstep and you maintain silence! But in the midst of my anger I stopped momentarily to ask what I was ready to do. I was, in fact, ready to do no more than my father. Earlier, he had said, "I knew the man only slightly. I don't think he was what you would call a troublemaker." My father, however, never wanted to believe that anyone could be a deliberate troublemaker, although some people did occasionally slip from the pedestal of decency. "But the man did seem to attract conflict," my father added. "He made people here restless (still does, for that matter), after that speech of his in church, and then his dying so soon afterward. I've heard a few good church members say that his death was nothing less than God's punishment for his disturbing our service. Not that I hold that view myself, but it does seem a weird coincidence that he should have this terrible death right after he spoke out against us."

I used that phrase when I talked to Alex Goodwin: "a weird coincidence." I asked if he thought that's what it was. He asked me if I'd talked to Tony Sauer, and when I said I had, he asked me what concern Jesse Christian was to me.

Too smugly, I quoted John Donne: "No man is an island," I said.

"Just answer the question," he said. And I told him that I'd known Tony a long time, and Jesse through Tony. "So you think Tony's telling the truth." I nodded. "And what are you doing about it?"

"That was going to be my question," I said.

"Why should it be yours any more than mine?" he asked. "I suppose you'd be quite relieved if I said I'd done nothing. You'd have your suspicions confirmed, that once again the church failed to take a stand on a moral issue. And at the same time you could sit back and think: Well, if he hasn't done anything, why should I?"

By that time I had lost all of my anger, maybe because he wasn't angry. He spoke calmly, like a father explaining to his son that disappointment is part of the fabric of this world. I stared at my shoes, sorry that I had come. But finally I had to ask him, "What did you do?"

And he said: "The first thing I did was write a resignation. The second thing I did was tear it up. Next I considered going to the sheriff and giving the law an opportunity to take its course. They deserve punishment, you know, because drunkenness does not convey the right to escape responsibility. But I hesitated because of Fernley. Such as he is, a weak, simpleminded, unreliable soul who couldn't quite master the eighth grade, he does have a mother who's getting old and who depends on him—not for financial support, certainly, but for emotional support: love, such as he can give. Oh, that may be a rationalization, to say that I feel sorry for an old lady and consequently feel that this outweighs all cries for justice. Well, call it what you will, but I was also afraid that even if this affair was brought into court, the evidence was so flimsy that

124

all three would be acquitted. Everything hung on Tony Sauer's testimony, and he admitted that he'd been drinking. Everyone knows that he's a frequent and heavy drinker. A good attorney could have turned him upside down.

"So what did I do? I went to see the guilty party, Howard Willson. And I told him the whole story, only leaving out Tony Sauer's name. I didn't tell him how I learned about the murder, I didn't even threaten to have the whole business taken to the law. He would have made short work of that, you know. But without bringing in the legal implications, I thought that I could rob him of any easy way out: I could keep it personal.

"I simply repeated the story as Tony gave it to me. And after I'd done that I didn't know what would come next, but I was scared stiff. Not of anything physical. I may have been naive, but I didn't think he would handle me the same way he handled Jesse, or that Indian. No, I was scared because in a way I was playing conscience—I was Nathan saying to David, 'You are the man'—and, you know, people don't like the church or her pastors to get that specific. It's all right to talk about the prophets just as long as you don't try to be one. And God knows that I wasn't particularly anxious to be a prophet, not outside that protective shell we call a pulpit. Right after I'd finished, the first thought that came to mind was: Well, I've said what I came to say, and now I guess I'll be going. I hope you have a pleasant day.

"As it was, though, I didn't say anything. And he laughed. It was not a very convincing laugh: short and sharp, suspended in the air like a kind of peace offering. All I had to do was reach up and take it and try it on for size, and everything would be forgotten. But I didn't laugh, I didn't try it on for size.

125

"So he sat back—we were in his office, overlooking the lake. Don and Dale were by the dock, getting a boat ready for some guests. 'I suppose,' he said, 'there are a lot of people in this town who resent success.'

" 'That's not the point, Howard,' I said. 'You egged those kids on, you took away their respect for other people . . . and in the process you took away their self-respect— and now they don't have respect for anything. They're like dogs now; they'll follow whatever scent is dragged in front of their noses.'

" 'So you believe that cockeyed story?' he said. 'Well, if you do, you're a damn fool.'

"I asked him then if he'd heard it before, and he said that he hadn't. I believe him. 'But you think it's possible, don't you?' I asked.

" 'I suppose anything is possible,' he said. 'But it doesn't mean anything until it's proved. And I don't think you could prove it if you tried the rest of your life.'

"I said, 'I'm not going to try to prove it. I'm just here to tell you what you've done—to your kids, and to Bill Fernley, and to Bremer Geare. They probably think they're heroes of some sort, slobbering dogs that you keep on a leash and turn loose from time to time for a little exercise.' I don't know what made me say that (shout it, actually) with no anger whatsoever, but instead a deep-down pain. All I wanted to do was talk about the weather, or about fishing or baseball, and there I was, playing the ghost of Jesse Christian, working to squeeze my way into his brain.

" 'I don't have to take that kind of talk,' he said.

" 'I know you don't,' I said. 'I've got no right to be here. But it is a little late to apologize, isn't it?' I got up to go, and he got up, too. It must have been a reflex action, one of those things you automatically do if you deal often with the public—anyway, he offered to shake hands with me. I stared at him, and he stared at his outstretched hand as though it belonged to someone else. 'Not yet,' I said. 'We're not ready to settle things that easily.'

"He dropped his hand, and he looked out the window again. 'All right,' he said, 'what do you want from me?'

"I said only one word; it floated out of me without my thinking about it or groping for it. 'Repentance.'

"If I had mentioned money, he would have known how to deal with me. I'm not sure that he even knew what repentance meant; I mean, he couldn't have given any kind of dictionary definition. But I do believe that he had a certain emotional grasp: he whispered, like a man right on the borderline of grief, 'Get the hell out of here.'

"I never see him in church anymore, although his wife comes occasionally. Don and Dale have left town; Mrs. Willson tells me that they're going to a trade school in Chicago, but whenever I ask for their address she tells me that she doesn't have it with her but will bring it the next time she sees me. Bremer Geare is gone too, to Los Angeles. Bill Fernley is still around, working at Larson's gas station, pretty much minding his own business, I guess."

"Do you ever see Howard Willson?"

"Oh yes, I see him now and then. In fact, he comes to see me, usually late on Saturday night, while I'm at the church working on my sermon. I always leave that until the last minute. He walks in and asks me what the sermon's going to be about. I tell him to come in the morning and find out. He says that he might just do that. And then he sits down, and we talk about a lot of things—confidential things that I really can't share with you. But I suppose you could say that in general we talk about whether life is worth living—like Shakespeare wrote, 'To be or not to be. . . .' It's an old story, you know; once a man has dabbled in death, created it, so to speak, for others, why, then, it's he himself who needs to be raised from it, to shake hands with life. Well, maybe for Howard Willson I'm a symbol—a rather tarnished one, but still a symbol—of life. And he reaches his hand out, and I still refuse to take it: 'Not now,' I say, or 'Not yet.' But that's not at all like saying, 'Never.' Three weeks ago Saturday night he came in, and we had a glass of wine together, communion wine, which would shock most of the parish. Well, so be it. We had a glass together, and he thanked me and left. We're not exactly warm friends, you see, but we're getting to the point where we can look each other in the eye and still say what we think."

And that was that. I don't think Alex Goodwin would have told me as much as he did except that he knew I was leaving soon. Maybe he had to talk to somebody, too.

Alex Goodwin said that it's an old story; it's an unending story: Alex and Howard Willson, Tony and the Indians that still find their way down to the lake shore and now use Jesse's house as a kind of retreat center, and now Dale Willson and I. I saw him in the mess hall three days ago; I greeted him, but we didn't shake hands—neither of us offered to. I asked him in passing how his brother was, and his father. He said he didn't know, he didn't keep in touch, he didn't care. Apparently he's cut the strings. And now he's here—to learn how to kill?

My father might say that it's a weird coincidence. I suppose it is. But a stronger voice than his asks me again: "What are you doing about it?"

I want to answer: "I've asked him how it feels to sleep with death, and if he's been able yet to wake up and live."

The unleashed dog with a taste for blood and a nose for death. And so I, too, am called to be Nathan—to start with Nathan, and hopefully to end as the angel who greeted the two Marys on their way to the tomb. God help me!

Coda

From the highway it looked like a college campus: autumn, gold and red, brief season in Minnesota, people carried their coats, walked, sat in the sun, lay back, looked up at the clear sky, crunched the crisp leaves, powdered them. "Yes," said Roger Sverd, "we have everything a college has."

They were inside, Main Hall, the lobby, ten of them, the five women in chrysanthemum colors, tired smiles, listening: the waning of a football weekend. Sverd pointed out the window, swept his hand across the landscape *magisterially*, thought Goodwin, tugging the clerical collar away from his chafed Adam's apple: *they are all mine, my sheep.*

"Dormitories, classrooms, gymnasium, library, even a lover's lane—quite unofficial, and well-patrolled, of course," Sverd smiled, holding it all in his palm *mine all mine.*

"Are you sure he's the superintendent?" Goodwin whispered to the man next to him. "Are you sure he doesn't belong here?"

"But the people in town," Sverd continued, "they still call it a nut house." The hand dropped; he shrugged. "That's why I'm always happy to see ministers, to explain to them what we're trying to do here. Because our job isn't one of incarceration, it's education! Now, you ministers know languages, I'm sure of that." *Speaking in tongues,* Goodwin thought, *like the rest of the nuts.* "And so you're aware that education has its roots in the Latin, and in the Latin it has the connotation of drawing out—as in, I suppose, the education of water, or drawing it out of the well."

"Like the education of the bladder," Goodwin whispered to his wife, who kicked him crisply in the ankle. Sverd went on: "That pretty well sums it up, what we're trying to do here: to draw these people up out of the darkness and into the light again. Well, now, and I guess that isn't so far from what you ministers are up to, bringing people to the light."

Hoskins, a Congregationalist, began to applaud. Alex Goodwin joined him, cupping his hands *sounds like cow droppings* and Pastor Mansell, self-described "solid Book of Concord no-nonsense one-hundred per cent Lutheran," scowled. Mansell had a brother here, alcoholic ward, no clapping for that. All the others joined in, having no relatives, only parishioners being drawn once again into the light, educated *Who are you here to see asked the woman in the reception room he gave the name friend or relative she asked neither parishioner* His hands fanned the air, collided *like cow droppings like we feed one another doing all of us so well feeding our sheep and so why do we have people here nuts* Sverd smiled, the applause slackened, one, two more plops from Alex.

"And now," Sverd said, "I'm sure you're anxious to make your calls—get to work, so to speak. But I want you to know, if there is anything that you can do to help us, any clues or suggestions that you can offer to make our treatment more effective and meaningful, we'd be very grateful if you'd tell us. We're all professionals here, that's the way I feel about it, professionals engaged in spreading the light. And I think it's a healthy sign whenever we share our insights"—Mansell walked out, Sverd stopped smiling, watched—"share our insights for the sake of these people whom we would like to turn back to your care just as soon as possible." Then he began to shake hands all around.

"It's probably our fault they're here in the first place," Hoskins said to Alex.

"There are some responsibilities," Alex answered, "that I will not shoulder, that being one of them."

"A typical Lutheran response," Hoskins said.

"We preach the Word—and let the chips fall where they may," Alex said.

"Come on," Laura Goodwin broke in. "We've got to see Dorothy Mae."

"Not until I convince Pastor Hoskins of the inestimable therapeutic value of my sermons."

"Just call me mister," Hoskins said.

"There, that's your problem," Alex said. "You're simply not convinced of the high calling to which you have been called."

"I don't need a clerical collar for security, if that's what you mean."

"I wear mine for penance," Alex said. "And to remind me what a damn fool I am."

"Maybe there's hope," Hoskins said.

"That brings us to another point," Alex said. "Why did Paul. . . ."

Laura tugged at his sleeve. "Come on, we've got to go."

"No," he said. "This is urgent. The point is, why did

Paul claim that love was greater than hope? Greater than faith—that I can understand. Even if it is a curiously Congregational concept. But personally I believe that it would be easier to live without love than without hope."

"It's just more speculation," Laura said. "And if you keep talking long enough, you won't have time to see Dorothy Mae."

"Well, for the sake of argument, I'll go along with Paul," Hoskins said.

"That's your free-church anti-institutional privilege," Alex said. "But you tell me which you'd rather be: a man in the grips of a hopeless love or a man with a bright hope of love?"

"Are you speaking sexually or spiritually?" Hoskins asked.

"Sexually," Laura said. "If he's being true to form." She pulled him away, and he blew Hoskins a kiss, skimmed past the handshaking Sverd, and they were out the door.

"That was rude," he said, "and besides, it's the duty of us Lutherans to tell the world what Paul really believed."

"It's your duty," Laura said, walking ahead of him, "to see Dorothy Mae. Now look for the Adams Recreation Center."

"Where the inmates are all bobbing for apples, no doubt," he said. "Well, there it is." He pointed to a small red brick building that looked like an elementary school, with gaily colored curtains and fall leaves scotch-taped to the windows *oh God I have nothing to say Hoskins and I Charlie McCarthy and Mortimer Snerd* "Try to be cheerful," Laura said.

Inside. "Dreams," she said: Miss Parker. Alice. Music teacher. Alma Center. Twenty-three years *now I am here we are all here making our lists,* thought Dorothy Mae.

"Dreams," said Miss Parker cheerfully, "are the language of the stars, the interior speech of astrology." Dorothy Mae did not look up, worked on her lists in her looseleaf notebook; Miss Parker, wearing her red silk Sunday dress and her two rhinestone rings and her single strand of pearls, sat across the table and rubbed at her liver spots and talked. "Dreams," she said, "tell us things. What do they tell you?"

At the top of the page *silly business I know it is and the doctors or somebody will ask to see it please not pushy or anything always please may I always may I please if you don't mind if it wouldn't be too much trouble oh how interesting a notebook and then you hand it over like you was in third grade I AM MAKING A GODDAMN LIST OF SOMETHING THAT I DON'T KNOW WHY THE HELL I AM MAKING THIS LIST only never like that but quietly politely the way Tony would want it I suppose the hell with Tony* "Grove Avenue." She printed it, neatly *it starts up by the greenhouse and cuts down past the hilltop park and runs around the edge of the hill turns east and ends in front of the hospital* At the top of the page, right under "Grove Avenue" she wrote: "East" on the left hand side of the page and "West" on the right. She paused, looked at the two words, scratched them out, replaced them with "Left" and "Right," looked again, scratched them out too.

"Loose teeth," said Miss Parker. "Have you ever dreamed of loose teeth?"

"Hmm?" Dorothy Mae looked up, looked back at the notebook, and wrote: "Up" and "Down" *down by the lake I have dreamed to the doctor running and running and going inches and someone chasing me I couldn't see and up toward the north away from the lake the first house down is Carlsons* She printed the name, "Carlson, Andrew," and underneath, indented, "Marva, Irene, John, Lawrence" *why the hell well is anybody writing down my name anywhere in this whole wide world is anybody putting down my address for all they know I could be* "Loose teeth," Miss Parker said, "are a sign of a loose connection, a fear of losing connections, breaking connection, breaking loose, unloosed moorings, unmoored and floating, no one anywhere knowing, everything loose and floating, tables and chairs and beds and dressers and chests and suitcases and trunks and stoves and frigidaires and bread boxes floating, and loose teeth are behind it all, you bet."

At least I know but she doesn't know at least what is my trouble is not everything flying off Miss Parker snatched the pencil from Dorothy Mae and threw it across the room. "Flying, floating, everything off the ground, don't you see? Oral Roberts says worse things than that are coming to pass at the end of the world, and we know it, dear, we know what it's all going to be like, we've had that dream about loose teeth." Dorothy Mae sighed, pushed back her chair, stood up, sighed again so that Miss Parker would not miss her weariness, and went to retrieve her pencil.

"Hello, Dorothy Mae," Laura said. Alex smiled, said hello, at least meant to say hello, but it came out as a melancholy croak.

"I'm a Pisces," Miss Parker shouted. "How about yourselves?" Laura smiled at her.

"I'm sorry," Laura said. "I don't know."

"Just ignore her," Dorothy Mae said.

Miss Parker beamed. "That's a bad sign—sure way to lose connections."

"I'm sorry." Laura smiled, turned to Dorothy Mae. "She's certainly . . . cheerful."

"She's crazy," Dorothy Mae corrected her. And then she walked out of the room and waited in the hall for the pastor and his wife. Miss Parker beamed, blinked, twisted her rings; Laura backed away, still smiling, and the pastor shoveled his hands into his pockets, looking for something, rattling coins and keys. "My notebook," Dorothy Mae said. The pastor pursed his lips and frowned. "My notebook," she repeated.

Miss Parker understood. She held up the notebook, held it aloft, as if she'd just scored a touchdown with it, toddled to the window with it, opened the window, and threw the notebook outside. "You wrote evil things about me, dear," Miss Parker said. "Evil and vicious things, that have a way of returning in the form of bad dreams." She spoke placidly, firmly but placidly: "Your teeth are going to fall out, dear. Don't say I didn't warn you."

Dorothy Mae dashed outside. Alex and Laura followed, after Laura waved an uncertain goodbye to Miss Parker. "What the hell. . . ." Alex said, half trotting, but with his hands still resolutely in his pockets. "Well," Laura whispered, "you can't expect things here to be perfectly *normal.*"

They were on the other side of the building. Dorothy Mae was peeling aside the shrubbery. Alex went to help, and it was he who found the notebook, wedged in the thorny crotch of a pyracanth, unkempt red bush that tore into his black suit and left several thin, dainty red lines on his hand. "Here," he said, gingerly extracting the notebook *here a sermon stigmatized by the spikes that crowned Jesus all for the sake of the sake of what* "I've got it." Dorothy Mae took it, at last smiled too, and he smiled back.

"Thank you," she said.

"What's in it?" he asked *tetanus shot* rubbing his
wounded hand *when since people have died from this
nothing more than a simple scratch what with poison on
every barb thorn needn't even be rusty the poison is invisible dirt doesn't tell one way or the other well two years
ago at least stepped on a nail at the beach but they aren't
good for more than that two years at best no medicine of
immortality is in itself immortal now there's a sermon
germ eucharistic sermon but who said it first Ignatius
Cyprian who'll know the difference anyway work in
tetanus bread wine and tetanus and poison at work within
us who can deliver us from this body of death tetanus can
a hair of the dog that bit us as if said Vaihinger but who
the hell is Vaihinger with as if philosophy never mind says
most of the world never mind but the evidence is somewhat in that the hair of the dog the dog is death the hair
of the dog well Jesus died became death so to speak comes
back again brings a hair of the dog drink it up now it all
begins to fit together as if said Vaihinger who is apparently
nobody in particular as if he was somebody who knew
what it was all about but the trouble is we are all doomed
to analogies as-if-ing all over the place*

*like the light in the library that flickered my whole
world flickered while I was reading Dreiser and I ask why
did I go into the ministry well it was a flickering light as
if it was a pure and holy call speak Lord thy servant
heareth as if the flickering light were not a dimming dying
neon tube dear God you can fool some of the people all of
the time and all of the people some of the time but not all
of the people all of the time our days are numbered and
we are all going to die as if that meant anything well peace
is a rare bird each man in his own wigwam and no more
war lions lambs birds of prey foxes and chickens with a*

new law engraved upon their hidden heart with a new feast before us Tony Dorothy Mae Laura and I those hapless kids Demeter Hager Willson Dorothy Mae here and many asleep in the Lord amen In both hands he held it, as if it were a service book, and absentmindedly he opened it, as if he were about to speak the Invocation, and Dorothy Mae, a little mouse in pain, squealed: "No, don't."

The first page, in guileless schoolgirl script:

CARVER COUNTY
Population, 23,412 (1960 census)
HALLMARK, city of
Population, 8,354 (1960 census)
HALLMARK STATE HOSPITAL
Population, about 1800 (said Doctor Troy)
BELKER COTTAGE
Population, 124 (by personal count)

Namely. Betty White, Alice French, Margaret Larson, Elizabeth Larson, Sarah Carter, Hannah Freed, Jane McGuire, Mary Gleason, Mary O'Brien, Frieda Jarnath, Claudia Clark, Jenny Mart, Sally Flanders, Edwina Flynn, Audrey Swanson, Elsa Gust, Anne Tibbetson, Thea Lodder, Beulah Marshall, Gertrude Peterson, Alda Peterson, Marjorie Distel, Carol Kline, Beth Anderson, Ingrid Swenson, Jewl Larson, Mary Leverton, Josephine Paris, Alice Trent, Sybil Mineer, Flora Gates, Lucille Gray, Alice Houston, Gen Cort, Dorothy Lester, Irene Carter, Millicent Griffith, Joy Rogers, Adele Carrithers, Vera Graves, Hetty Sage, Jane Corrigan, Margeret Gower, Selena Ransom, Estelle Aubrey, Norma Adams, Alberta Perkins, Leah Johnson, Faith Albright, Maude Lange, Constance Lee, Francis Cross, Elvira Barrington, Betty Clawson, Virginia Meade, Ruth Nielson, Eleanor Hayden, Lucy Townsend, Barbara Trowbridge, Helen Larson, Catherine Bender, Rachel Carter, Helen Everson, Ruth Paulsen, Mary Jane Flagler, Veronica Gratz, Georgia Niemeyer, Jesse

I am Dorothy Mae Nelson on second floor section D third bed on right

HELLO, I AM_____

WHO ARE YOU??????????????????????

"It's mine," she said, very simply, and put out her hand. He closed the book, passed it to her, and said, "Tony asked me to see you" *because he died was killed succumbed cashed in his chips took the ten count dust to dust ashes to ashes in sure and certain hope of the* She walked away; they followed her: not back into the recreation building—they walked down one of the paths. "Sometimes," he said, saying no more; she walked a pace ahead of them, and they followed *we are sick because we want to be sick lacrimae rerum we get wrapped up in his dying as if again as if as if there is no getting away from it as if we were staring into the world's navel seeing the beginning of everything in the beginning there is this this knotted veil*

"Well, what am I going to do?" Tony asked Alex: "There she sits and we can't get her to eat" *As if there was an answer* "I mean, what's there to do? Nobody's going to marry her, what with her mouth hanging open like that, she looks like she's been kicked in the face, and nobody wants something like that around, unless it's somebody who wants to keep kicking her in the face." They were in Alex's office, Alex behind the desk, Tony fidgeting, untying his shoelaces, tightening them, tying them, crossing to the window, tentatively touching the crucifix by the door, running his raspy fingers over the near-naked body: corpus: "At one time I thought maybe he was interested."

"Jesse?"

"The two of them got along, she liked him; well, more than that, more than just liked him. And I guess I encouraged her. I didn't discourage her, anyway."

"Yes, there were some who talked about that."

"Because he was black."

"Yes, that pretty well sums it up."

"My wife was against it too. She didn't like the idea of her sister living with a colored man. But I said, 'How much dignity have we got to lose?' He was the only one, really. She's ugly; hell, you might as well say it. She's got a face like a sick horse. And I don't say that because I don't like her. But the fact is that you don't ever get used to it, you don't ever completely forget that she's . . . she's ugly. It was his dignity; he was the one with some dignity to lose. He was his own man, he could come and go as he pleased, no strings attached—except if he took her along. As far as he was concerned, she was strictly bad news."

"Maybe," Alex said, "he didn't think so."

"He never said, one way or the other."

"But the problem now is that she won't eat," Alex said.

They followed her, the two of them, Alex and Laura, and she walked on, holding the book to her breast *as if a procession we should be singing singing Holy Holy Holy lift up your heads o ye gates and cast down your crowns around the glassy sea* "No," Tony said, "it's not just that she won't eat. She calls me up, too."

"Calls you up?" Alex repeated.

"She'll go out after supper some nights, and about half an hour later the telephone'll ring and I'll answer it and this voice will tell me to go up the lake road because somebody wants to see me. The first time I thought it was for real, and I went. I walked up the road, up to where Jesse was killed. There was a wind that night, and the leaves were rustling. It was like a moaning, like somebody was hurt and moaning, and I don't know if it was the leaves or if it was Dorothy Mae. I called her name, and the moaning just got louder, and I began to think it was a ghost, and I ran all the way home, just like a scared rabbit. I asked Dorothy Mae the next morning if she called, but she shook her head that she didn't. But I keep getting these phone calls two, three times a week, always when she's out. I don't ask her anymore. And she doesn't say."

"What does your wife think?"

"At first I told her about it and I said that I thought it was Dorothy Mae. But she didn't think Dorothy Mae would do such a thing. Anyway, when she calls now I tell my wife it was a wrong number."

"Does she believe that?"

"Probably not. But it's easier for her to say she does than to deny it's Dorothy Mae." Tony walked to the window, pressed his head against the glass. "She thinks. . . ."

"Who thinks?" Alex cut in.

"Dorothy Mae thinks . . . she thinks that it was my fault he was killed."

"Has she said so? In so many words?"

"Two days ago she ate an egg. Since then, nothing. Except a glass of water, a cup of coffee."

"That's not going to kill her," Alex said.

"Look!" he said, crossing to the desk, pushing his face over the no-man's-clutter of church bulletins and stewardship blurbs until the muscles in his neck flexed, tense, cords as true as steel. "She's not just a sack!" He raised his right hand, formed a fist, Alex flinched, and the fist crashed through the insubstantial paper: "I know she's not going to die. But she's not living, either. She's getting sick, like she was before. And I don't know what the hell to do about it" *Should have said come to church bring the family* The sky was red as the red trees, the air was cooler now, the ground held no warmth this season, and they walked on *healing words therapy yes where the hell is it where the heaven we can get desperate man can turn that way desperate in the eye of that knotted veil this man*

141

*pastor in Kandiyohi took out the joke book my husband
the lady said is not satisfying me and I am afraid weak of
other men oh yes yes yes my goodness take your mind off
it what you need is a laugh Tony give her a laugh and
communion first Sunday of every month* "Maybe," Alex
said, groping *better at burying than healing buried him
well without a hitch never miss hurl down the clods thudding on the box* HOLLOW-SOUNDING HOLLOW
THOCK THOCK THOCK *trinitarianly thudding*
"Maybe you should take her to the doctor."

Finally: "Where are we going?" Laura asked.
Without looking back, Dorothy Mae answered: "Visiting hours are over at six."

The next time they met was in Staley's Restaurant, three
weeks later. Alex was in the back booth, alone, having
coffee. Tony walked in, Alex noticed him and called his
name. The waitress came and Alex ordered two cups of
coffee and two doughnuts. "I've missed you," he said.
"Where?" Tony asked. "In church?"
"Don't you think I know who's there and who isn't?"
Tony dunked his doughnut, sucked the coffee out. "It's
nothing personal," he said. "But to tell the truth, I don't
give a care whether you miss me in church or you don't."
"I'm glad it's nothing personal."
"There's nothing to it, that's why I don't go," he said.
He dunked the doughnut again and sucked it noisily.
Alex watched him, watched them both in the mirror across
the room, two men drinking coffee in a small-town restaurant. "There's nothing to it," he repeated, "because it
doesn't change anything. Look at them: Willson, Hager,
the lawyer, they all sit there. . . .

"Not Willson. . . ."

"He's sat there like the rest of them. I saw him. Just sat there, that's what they did. And it isn't as comfortable as staying in bed. And the Sunday paper is more entertaining. Or else going out fishing. Or hunting. But still they come. God knows why—force of habit for some of them, and some just plain like you, and some are scared of hell and they want to be reminded it's going to be all right for everybody who fears and loves the lord. Well?"

"Well?"

"Am I wrong?" he asked, looking contemplatively at the last bite of doughnut.

"You don't seem to think so," Alex said, watching them in the mirror.

"I'm waiting to be shown, that's all," Tony said. "I'm waiting for Willson and Hager to show me. I'm waiting for the lawyer to make some arrests and forget his damn political career."

"Maybe if they did change . . . if they *could* change, then there'd be no reason for them to come back." He stopped; new words formed on his lips, but his tongue refused to release them *for sinners that's what the church is for we forgive thieves murderers come one come all be what you are and that means be not just* "I know," he said finally, "what you're talking about."

"You couldn't have stomached Jesse."

"No," Alex said. "Once was enough."

"Of course," Tony said, "we're no better."

"We're too scared . . . no, not scared, too ineffective to expect miracles."

Tony peered into his cup. "He stood up," Tony said.

"And you don't?"

Still peering, looking for something beneath his own

143

muddy reflection: "Dorothy Mae went to Hallmark yesterday," he said. "I signed the papers. I called the sheriff, and we had a quick hearing with the doctor. I signed the papers, it didn't take more than a day and a half . . . just a matter of writing my name wherever the sheriff marked a little *x*. And then the sheriff put her in his car. He drove, and his wife sat on the other side, and Dorothy Mae was in the middle. And off they went. To Hallmark."

"Because she wouldn't eat?" *like doing away with a puppy who couldn't be housebroken no not exactly who wouldn't do the same thing the sick need a physician the sick who are well yes who are unable to eat the doughnut drink the coffee look in the mirror and give a name to what they see when we should be beating our breasts the two of us muttering here yes he did the right the only thing he did I would who wouldn't amen* "Or," as an afterthought, "did something else happen?"

"I was watching television the other night," Tony said. "I fell asleep on the davenport. But I woke up when I heard something in the kitchen. The lights were off and at first I thought it was just one of the cats. Then I heard a drawer open and I heard the silverware rattling. It crossed my mind this was a burglar, but who'd want to steal our silverware? Just the same, I figured you never know what people might want to steal these days, so I kept quiet. Pretty soon the drawer was closed and I could see this figure coming toward me. I closed my eyes until I could feel somebody standing over me. I opened my eyes just wide enough to peep out, and I saw it was Dorothy Mae. I started to jump up and she came down on me. All of a sudden it was as clear as day what she got in the kitchen. It was a knife. With my body I was trying to get out of the way, but my mind said to me, as calm as you please,

'She's going to kill me.' And down she tumbled, her fist came crashing into my chest, right over my heart. I figured I was dead, that's all there was to it. I was dead. Except that she didn't have a knife, just a fist, an empty fist. I tried to push her away with my hand. . . ." He unbuttoned his right sleeve as he talked and rolled it up, as if he were going to show Alex an old vaccination. "See, look here," he said. "She bit me. She snarled at me, like a dog, and she bit me." The teethmarks were plain; the skin had been broken, not merely broken but sliced through, so that the hunk of flesh was practically unattached, lay there by the grace of gravity and a few thin strings of skin, a white island surrounded by a flaming red sea, a dead violated island reeking of alcohol, puffy and diseased.

"You better see a doctor about that," Alex said.

"My body's used to it . . . fish hooks and splinters and everything," Tony said.

"But not bites," Alex said. "My God, you could get blood poisoning."

He rolled down the sleeve. "Why do you think she did it?" Alex shook his head.

"I ran into our bedroom and I showed my wife," he went on. "And I said the first thing that came into my mind: 'She tried to kill me,' I said. 'I'm sending her away.' And once I heard myself say it, I couldn't think of anything else to do. I was afraid of her. And do you know why?" Again Alex shook his head. And Tony leaned over the table, spilling his coffee, and Alex watched the coffee soaking into the shirt, staining it as dark as if it were more blood, and Tony whispered: hissed it, as one who is not accustomed to whispering: "Because I deserved it."

"Deserved it?"

145

He smiled, forced a smile of weary fierceness, like a small, trapped animal anxious to prove to all, most of all to himself, that he still has one weapon left: "Do you think I deserved something better?" The smile tightened. "Or worse?"

At last—"All right, I'll go to see her," Alex said.

"I never asked you to," Tony said.

"Then what were you asking me to do?" Alex asked.

"I thought we were just having a cup of coffee together," Tony said. "I didn't think it was a matter of asking for anything."

They left together, walked off in opposite directions. Alex went to the post office: a bill for communion wine *ought to make our own symbolically effective look up recipes tomorrow* a letter requesting a transfer for Mary Schiller nee Olson *who in hell is she half of Nortonville is Olsons some dead soul suddenly revived strangely warmed by the First Baptist Church of Conover why would they write for transfer have to baptize all over again anyway* he wadded it into a loose ball and threw it into the wastebasket, stared at it, floating on the top of a sea of Rexall 1¢ Sale flyers, and retrieved it *strangely warmed ready to believe anything monks levitating in prayer the dead revived fortunetellers Mary Schiller nee Olson converted help my unbelief* a revised Thanksgiving worship from the commission on worship and church music *twelve flowers on the altar for twelve apostles worship vastly meaningful when done properly no flowers during Advent no weddings better let them sleep in sin than disturb church year form is all strangely warmed by this crap believe everything believing all things fit together the foolish all foolish things monstrous things grotesque flowers Mary Schiller nee Olson a mad lady who bites* "Yes," Alex said, flipping the revised Thanksgiving worship folder into the wastebasket; "Yes," to no one in particular *take and eat this is my body given for you this food in the wilderness cannibals are sometimes by custom sometimes by necessity nothing else having to eat nothing but the invitation this is take eat Capernaitic eating bloody meal no not that was Jesus' mind say smartass Germans I believe everything help my unbelief Dorothy Mae needs take eat what is given for you for whom the Lord sends believing everything monks rolling in prayer on the ceiling Mary Schiller nee Olson rescued from the basket by strangely warmed baptists in this wilderness Lord provides real blood not just a matter of believing those bodyless wafers the deaconesses make in Omaha sometimes a person needs a real bite to feed the fury see Thomas real bite bloody real take and eat bless the cannibals believing they take and eat feed my sheep* he tossed away, unopened, a circular advertising the *American Anthropological Review,* and another one from the Friends of Ralph Ginzburg for Free Speech in American Letters, and, final item, opened a letter from Paul Westfield postmarked "Winter Beach, South Carolina." Plain white paper, typing paper, and pencil *why me* "Dear Pastor" *in trouble confession pregnant girl absent without leave kind of letters pastors receive still he's the one the one I talked too much to said too much* "It seems a long, long way from basic training. I think I mentioned to you while I was home that I was going to be in school, tech training—they think I have the right aptitude to become a radio operator; the right aptitude, not necessarily the right attitude. Anyway, it's a not entirely unpleasant life at the base, very little drill, six hours of class, and maybe an hour or two of study at night, waiting, waiting for the two years to be over.

"Right now, though, I've got a weekend pass and I'm taking advantage of the sunny southland, in a motel in Winter Beach about fifty yards from the ocean, nothing but sleeping, reading, sunning for a couple of days, playing the millionaire playboy in a $4.98 swimming suit" *nothing but yes I'll bet nothing but until after dark when comes the subliminal flood I remember not that old myself I remember yes give them lectures on vd films of chancrous old vets feed my sheep*

"However, I'm not writing simply to make you envious of sun, sand, and wave" *yes now it comes is no one strangely warmed these days bolster us up one another feed me no never that I thirst he drinks* "You probably heard from my parents or maybe Howard Willson that Dale Willson and I went through basic together, even though we didn't see much of each other. Then he was assigned to radar school, so I supposed that whatever relationship there was between us was over. The worst of it is that I never really decided, or discovered, what that relationship consisted of. Priest and confessor? There's too much arrogance when I use those words. Maybe they're saved for you and Howard Willson *am I blushing embarrassed I can't tell the difference between compliment and facetiousness no it's simply that I know the truth I said intimated hinted all that sinisterly Willson thinks of suicide murderer whose deed murders his own conscience well what is the truth Pilate the truth is I believe everything aerial monks the works working my imagination feverishly he visits me yes so far the truth we share some wine he fishes with me fishes for me always angling for how much I know using his own guilt as bait too bad he said too bad about Christian yes too bad I said and he said some people don't think it was an accident no I said I don't think it was either one little little word will fell him one little dart yes Howard your sons did it your sons because they are your sons because you are their father because it is all wrapped up together they fed on you they fed on bile and they committed murder I know it all and the truth is I will stand up stand up for Jesus but not for this one bloody chunk of justice chew the bread and share this Mogen holy David but no flesh no blood no thanks no blood let it spill the truth is I can drive up the lake road now past that spot and never consider could play hide-and-seek in the dusk on Golgotha if given the chance test me Lord I am capable of all insidiousness no blatancy your perfect humble willing obedient servant yes the truth is he comes to see me and we drink wine not blood and never look at our hands we know what we are and lack the courage to speak it Hager knows it too good deacon and Albertson name them my pillars we know it we have this world we leave it to you now even my heart disavows I am not that bad have opened my holy bottle if we cannot stand blood we have this wine at least this memorial we remember in not remembering have a little mercy this world that rots like dead flesh on dead bones this world we hand over hoping it hangs together until we've done the job of turning over this world we know is rotten we know what we've made we still hope we still dream it won't fall unfleshed off dry bones we hope damn it drink our wine and hope we knew one good not remembering we remember blush if only we could speak it fall all of us into each other's arms and not for once tear asunder remembering yes remembering this flesh this flesh is that all we can do stand aside is that all remembering this flesh must be torn and speak it as if as if more than memorying we have here in our glasses hope "With us* anyway, with Dale and me, the only words that seem to fit are antagonist—no, there's just one word, just antagonist, no protagonist. We just antagonize, we can't help one another. And now I guess I'd let the whole matter drop, I never knew Jesse Christian that well, I'm as innocent as the next man—but, to tell the truth, I'm also a bit sick of being innocent. Oh, I imagine that according to the catechism I struggled through some years ago, I'm as sin-ridden as the next man—and yet it strikes me now that the sin we talked about when we were getting ready for confirmation is actually pretty small potatoes, the sort of stuff the Catholics would throw under the category of scrupulosity. And I'm a big boy now, and I'd like to think that I'm ready for some of the big sins, the kind that burn away innocence and even leave some lasting scars. That sounds pompous. I wouldn't say it, wouldn't write it down, except that here he is again. Dale Willson. I was walking down the beach last night, a few hours after I got here, and I saw a convertible pull up to the hotel next to mine—the grand hotel, the Winter Towers, out of my class, and maybe I'm bitter about that—anyway, Dale Willson got out of the convertible and went into the Winter Towers. I haven't seen him since, don't have to see him at all, in fact. But the point is, should I?

"Confront. That's the word. Pour poison into his ear? No, that's what the evil uncle did to Hamlet's father. I want to play Hamlet, lay bare the sins of the murderer. Even if it means dying. Aye, there's the rub, isn't it? Dying. I want a drastic confrontation without any drastic repercussions. And I don't know how or if I'll handle it.

"And that's all there is. No climax here at all, just a boy simmering in his innocent juices. Or his lusts. I don't know which. I only want to tell you that the story isn't over. We're not home yet. Maybe never will be. You see—confession time now, even if it is old hat for you—no, on second thought, forget it, a pack of little sins to mask the large obscene innocence. And then the worst sin of them all—my posturing, which is nothing to confess. Yes, that's it, my worst sin is that I have nothing to confess. Maybe I can make some progress this week."

He signed the letter "Sincerely," addressed the envelope, stuffed it and sealed it, held it as if to tear it in two, then put on the stamp and went into the lobby to mail it. It was five o'clock. He returned to his room, showered, laid out his clothes: new, everything new; navy blue stockings fitting lightly, firmly over his calves, navy blue sansabelt slacks, powder blue oxford-weave button-down shirt, Italian silk tie, red with blue fleur-de-lis pattern, white linen jacket with blue pin stripe, calfskin oxfords that buckled on the side. On the top of the dresser there was a clutter of straight pins, cardboard, tissue paper, price stickers and tags; he swept all of it into the wastebasket, took one long look at himself in the mirror on the bathroom door, dropped the key into his pocket, checked once more in the mirror to see that the key lay flat, left, closed the door.

He had no car, took a Greyhound from the base, three and a half hours, return ticket in his wallet; he ate in the restaurant adjoining the motel: salad with roquefort dressing, deep-fried shrimp, au gratin potatoes, parkerhouse rolls, apple pie a la mode, two cups of coffee; he read the *Charlotte News,* the sports section twice. He left a fifty-cent tip, paid his check, three twenty-five. It was only six-thirty.

On the bus he had passed an amusement park; he walked back to it, about two miles. The park occupied an entire block, except for a sculptured concrete building that resembled two scoops of peach ice cream; ringing the second scoop was an endless neon tube whose curlicues read, over and over, "dancedancedancedancedancedance." He entered, deposited a quarter into a "Do-It-Urself Photo Booth," and had six pictures of himself in sixty seconds. He examined the stalls on the first floor: water ice, tasti-freeze, funny hats, plastic masks, canes, windup dolls, balloons, perpetual-motion water-sipping ostriches, kosher hot dogs, chocolate-covered bananas, comic buttons, souvenir ashtrays and pillowcases, native seashells, live turtles and baby alligators shipped anywhere, saltwater taffy, anklets and bracelets personally engraved, American flags and patriotic bumper stickers, choice of forty different college sweatshirts in all sizes, religious wall plaques, ceramic statuettes of Presidents Kennedy and Johnson, genuine artificially aged reproductions of the U.S. Constitution and the Declaration of Independence, Confederate flags, dashboard statues of Jesus and St. Francis, periscopes and telescopes made in Hong Kong, beach towels, beach balls, beach umbrellas, beach pails, beach toys, transistor radios, transistor phonographs, long-playing records, mother-of-pearl rosaries, sandals made in Mexico, jasmine-scented candles, miniature plaster of paris bas-reliefs of Michelangelo's Last Supper, popcorn, potato chips, Crackerjacks, Krispee Korn, Fudgees, Bacon Crisps, Creem Goodies, Kwik Kurls, Ice Delites, Mammoth Maltees, bikini nighties, floppy straw hats, live chameleons sold each one with his own leash. He bought a button for fifty cents.

VENI
VIDI
WEEWEE

He put it into his pocket and went upstairs. There was a band playing, the Conquistadores, three electric guitars, saxophone, drums. From the ceiling was suspended a large ball whose surface was thousands of tiny mirrors, and as the ball revolved it caught and played back the light from four spots, red and blue and green and yellow. The only other light came from the neon tube outside, shining through the parallel windows that ringed the room "ecnad-ecnadecnadecnadecnadecnadecnad." The amplifiers were turned up, but there were hardly more than a dozen dancers on the floor. It was very hot, and the bar opposite the stairs was busy. Paul walked along the wall to the bar, waited his turn, asked for a bottle of beer.

"Only soft drinks, son," the man said.

Paul shook his head, watched the band for a few minutes, noticed it was five minutes to eight, left.

In the amusement park there were: the Merry-Go-Round, the Tiny Tot Cars, the Tiny Tot Boats, the Tiny Tot Choo-Choo, the Tilt-a-Whirl, the Rocket, the Ferris Wheel, the Snake, Doctor Fantastico's Hall of Mirrors, the World's Largest Mechanical Orchestra, the Rapi-Dive, the Vampire's Revenge, the Shaker, Guess Your Age and Weight, the Milk Bottle Throw, the Penny Pitch, the Ring Toss, the Balloon Buster, the Shooting Gallery, the Wheeler-Dealer, Mister MekaNiko and Twin—Which One's the Machine? Each place had its own neon frame, as though everything were being observed through an X-ray machine, and the neon was the hard bone, what remains after the insubstantial has been cut through—and then the sluggish, diaphanous insects, some larger than hummingbirds, multitudinous species, clotted around the lights of the ticket booths, and then the whirring of wings, the humming of the neon. He watched, passed along; at

eight minutes to nine he was at the bar in the Hurricane
Lounge of the Winter Towers.

Drinking his second scotch and soda *unaccustomed as
I am go slow he will be herewill herewith face in the bar-
room floor across a crowded room enchanted so good to
see you arrest this man officer murder in the first degree
wrap him in the flag sink him deep fathoms fifty food for
the fish why am I here back tomorrow on three o'clock bus
so much fun so much fun fun fun to sit in this bar and
drink alone and listen why South Carolina cannot field
winning football big man taken seriously encircles his
drink like a lobster red lobster in the face redneck next
to me blonde blue-eyed Nordic god masterracer one-
seventy tan not handsome well handsome is as handsome
images masterracing Hitler thought he was handsome maybe handsome in the mirror there stare at him iceself weak
mouth ouch! damn button in the appendix* he shifted on
the stool, reached into his jacket pocket and flipped the
button so the pin was facing out, pushed his empty glass
forward and the bartender replaced it with a full one *dear
pastor here I am gentlemanly here with this here socker-
ment sock it down full of loaving for the hole human raze
boy in the mirror familiar I know that boy boy miceself
boy if I see him boy in this tender bar pastor exuding tend-
erness bar none John the story goes pastor one of the old
Johns pelted untenderly by crap of the world stood up
held up by two of the beartenders borne up arms out like
a cross where did I hear this you or college old story he
stood up on his least legs little children he said love one
another the least of these leased yes him too the most handsome of all yes he said in Stob's underage Stob never asked
tenderly yes he said the two of us happening along we happened how's school and there was Stob's yes he said we*

*sipped quietly tenderly bars down sipped Saturday heroes
four five blocks away cavorting all this was nearly mine he
never said yes he said I am a kind of whore I take money
from Hager saved enough earned enough took bus to California this summer to see her yes I saw her followed her
watched her* "Damn it," said the red lobster enveloping
his drink, "those guys sit in Columbia and wait! They
think a kid has got some kind of natural loyalty. Hell, I
don't care how much a kid loves South Carolina, when
these recruiters drive up to his home from Atlanta or
Chapel Hill or Alabama and they ask him how he'd like
to take their Caddy out for a spin and maybe have a weekend visiting the campus, *including* a little sex play with
the campus queen—well, I ask you, how the hell much
loyalty does he feel toward little old South Carolina? Those
bums in Columbia send him a sweatshirt and figure they've
done the boy a big favor. That ain't the way to handle
recruiting, not if you want to build a dy-nas-tee. Now you
tell me, is that the truth or is that the truth?" *truth is never
said hello watched listen he said sipping tenderly glory
passing four five blocks away blocking tackling touchdowns
faint cheers winning the day ski-u-mah going gophers I
was at this party drinking sisters and brothers Greeks
sneaks hollow horses whores worse to bed in bedroom
philosophically speaking prone to philosophy prone going
hollow horse we two Greeks horsed into readying hands
ready seeking she asked philosophically prone what is love
I said yes love is faithfulness all it broke horse cracked
open we tumbled back to booze one garden for my seed
is that truth I asked truth he asked Jesus savior pilate me
truth is yes and no love is yes and no is faithfulness yes
I said faithfulness this Greek she backed away I burned
she fled love is faithfulness not necessarily the lovers oh*

pastor I ache for Greek bearing gift hollow gift and love he said yes I went to see her saw where are the Greeks hello hello hollow yes he said waiting I know this garden know my hollowness hello I ached to say and couldn't the rest came running in Greeks baring news of the game ski-u-mah rah rah rah victory victory now faithfulness he said hmm I said faithfulness he said why in hell did I ever game over they piled in thirstily why in hell did I ever he said I said hmm say that he said why did I say that hmm I said never mind he said can't hear yourself game's over who won I said who knows he said still thinking about it yes said mirror looking the boy there lobster next in back entering the seersucker suit "I don't give a damn what the rules are; if you want a football team you got to go out and get a football team, because it don't come to you" *tan collegiate holding the chair for* pushed the glass forward and the bartender replaced it with a full one *holding the chair beehive hair pale sits rummages for cigarette waits he sits too match flickers flame smoke Dale Willson* "The point is," lobster said, "you don't get into a horse race just for the sake of running. That ain't so complicated."

They sat, he stared into the mirror. The waitress took their order. Neither of them spoke; she smoked, let the smoke curl out of her nostrils, he took out a bill and laid it on the table, between them, she glanced at the bill, at him, then looked away. She had high cheekbones, close-set eyes, Grecian nose, not too large, almost but not quite, still large enough that it lifted her face, was the beginning point for the graceful arabesque that swept from her flared nostrils like a relaxed spring, then proudly ascended the bridge, eased over and around the cheekbones and flowed, gently curving, down her Nefertitian neck. Her mouth was thin, a straight, disapproving line, an economic geometry at odds with the superfluous grace of the rest of her; long bare arms, too, and high lean breasts. She wore black, unadorned, and a white knitted stole over her shoulders. When their drinks arrived, he handed hers to her, said something, smiled broadly. She replied, as if from a great height, great lady priorly engaged in some consuming ritual.

Paul's drink was half gone. He slipped down from the stool and weaved across the room. He bumped into several people, caused one woman to spill part of her drink on the floor—"Clumsy!" she snapped at him, turned to her companions. "He isn't a day over twenty." Hearing, Paul stopped, spoke over his shoulder, "Defen'ing your country, ma'am; first in war, first in peach. . . ," giggled, walked on. Dale Willson, expressionless, marked his coming with a curt nod.

"Hello, you old Minnesotan," Paul said.

"What have you been celebrating?" he asked.

"Your great good fortune," Paul said, setting his drink on their table; "your fortune being able to stay in this sumchus mansion. But I suppose in your father's house there're many mansions."

"What the hell are you talking about?"

He sat down in the extra chair. "I see you have a guest."

"That's what it looks like," Dale said.

"Yes," Paul said, lifting his glass as if to toast, "it certainly is what it looks like. It looks like you have a guest."

"Let's finish up and get out of here," he said to the woman.

"Do you know him?" she asked.

"I used to know him," he said.

"Birds of a feather," Paul said. "We used to sit on the same limb."

"Are you both from Minnesota?" she asked.

"Everybody in the world is from Minnesota," Paul said.

"Sure, that's right," Dale said, pushing his chair back. "We'll talk about that sometime."

"Just a minute now," Paul said. "This is important. Right?" He looked at the woman; she sighed, sipped her drink. "Right! Because the beginning of the world is in Itasca State Park, where gushes forth the mighty Mississippi, father of waters. Do you believe that?"

"Sure," she said, testing a smile. "If you say so."

"Let's get out of here," Dale said, taking hold of her arm. But she pulled away from him.

"I'm not your property," she said. "And I don't like to be pushed around."

"Amen!" Paul said. "And that's the truth. Which's got its beginning in the mighty Mississippi."

"What do you know about the truth?" she asked him. This time she seemed interested, set her glass down, leaned forward.

"He doesn't know a damn thing about the truth," Dale said. "He's drunk. Now let's get upstairs."

"There's no hurry," she said, without looking at him. "You're not going to take that long anyway."

"What's your name?" Paul asked her.

"Souzanna," she said. "With an s-o-u. It's Greek. The Greeks know all about truth."

"I know the Greek word for sea," Paul said.

"You know a lot of things you don't know nothing about," Dale said. To Souzanna: "He's a soldier, just like me. We were in basic together. He's a college boy, he knows everything. Like the night he found this comic book in the barracks." Now they were all leaning forward, three conspirators *Sad Sack it was picked it up well I said here's manual of arms for the illiterate* "He held it up and he said, 'Well, this man must be bucking for Officer Candidate School.' He figured—he was so smart, you see—he figured the only ones in the barracks was himself and a couple of his buddies. But there was also this boy from Tennessee who owned the comic book, he was over six foot and over two hundred pounds, and he picked up little Paul here and he carried him out in back and he said, 'Here, you either eat this comic book and pay me for it or I'll pound the . . . the tar out of you.' " Dale grinned, immensely pleased. "The brave American fighting man," Paul said, "searching for truth" *why didn't he say it the way it was pound the tar he pays for a lady going to treat her for a lady touching good soldier touching he moves me pound the tar he talks to her to me too to me I'm here he didn't pay for me no didn't pay hasn't paid me off either bad debt here yes pound the tar you pounded the tar that's where we are* "And so he didn't say a word, he ate the comic book, down on his hands and knees, he ate it up, piece by piece."

"Only two pages," Paul said. "I only did it because I believe that a man's tar is his own private property. Nobody's got a right to mess around with another man's tar. Of course, maybe that's what we've got tar for, just for other people to mess around with, that's just a possibility too, you might say."

"You keep talking, boy, I might find some more of that comic book for you to eat."

"What is the Greek word for sea?" Souzanna asked, mother petting her youngest son, inquiring, confidently, whether he can spell refrigerator: now do your best trick.

"Thalassa," he said, happily. *"Thalassa, thalassa, thalassa."*

"Who in hell cares?" Dale snorted.

"The Greeks," Paul said. "When they made the big march up country."

"When was that?" Souzanna asked.

"I don't know," Paul said. "I don't know where they were coming from or where they were going, but they went wild when the first ones saw the sea, and they said, 'Pass it along, *thalassa, thalassa*,' and so it went down the line from soldier to soldier and somehow they knew they were going to make it back home. What they saw, actually, was the mighty Mississippi."

"He doesn't know what the hell he's talking about," Dale said.

"Pass it along," Paul said, loudly now; "we ought to share it—*thalassa, thalassa*"—he began to giggle, stood up, called out, *"Thalassa, thalassa,* think about it folks; we're on the way."

"Shut up, you damn fool," Dale said, rising to pull him down. He reached over the table, clutched Paul's sleeve in his fist: "Sit down," he hissed.

Paul stopped giggling, put his hand over Dale's fist— "Did he puke on you?" Dale's eyes opened wide, he said nothing. "That's what happens, doesn't it? Did he puke on you?" Dale said nothing, stared. "Did he puke his tar all over you? Maybe you're all black inside your clothes— aren't you afraid to have a woman see that?" Dale pushed him back suddenly and he fell into his chair. Their neighbors were eyeing them uneasily. Paul raised his hand, grasped some invisible wire, and pulled himself to his feet again:

"That's what it's all about, folks. *Thalassa, thalassa.* Pass it along, the mighty Mississippi's just around the bend, Itasca, clean water; it all starts in a spring."

Dale, still standing, pulled Souzanna to her feet. "We're getting out of here."

"Wait!" Paul pushed the small table aside and the glasses smashed on the floor. He fished into his pocket for the button, took it out and pinned it on Dale's jacket:

VENI
VIDI
WEEWEE

"First annual *thalassa* award," he said "—entitles the recipient to one genuine bottle of Mighty Mississippi Spring Water and . . . and . . . ." He heard a small patter of applause; it was Souzanna, and he acknowledged her, raised his arms as if to implant a benediction. Then Dale hit him. Meant for the chin, the first punch landed on the shoulder; the second, a left jab, grazed Paul's ear, and the right shot in again, flush on the mouth. By that time the lobster had stepped in; with a claw in each collar, he nearly raised them off the floor as he whisked them out of the lounge, down the lobby and out the door that led to the swimming pool. "There, maybe you can cool off," he said as he spun them to the ground. He roared with laughter, apparently full of appreciation for his wit, and returned to the lobby. Souzanna was there—the two of them, Paul and Dale, could see her in the doorway, could see the lobster stop to say a few words to her. She linked her arm in his and went with him back to the lounge.

Slowly Paul sat up, tested for missing teeth with his tongue, wiped the blood from his chin with the back of his hand. And Dale came after him again, swarmed over

161

him, hitting fiercely, wildly, hitting out, flailing, with his eyes closed. Paul squirmed away and ran toward the beach. On the sand he tripped over a toy pail and Dale leaped on him again. He did not hit this time, but straddled his body, pinned down his arms, and spat in his face. "Why did you have to say that?" he cried out. "I never did nothing to you." Paul looked up at him, and he could not tell whether it was sweat or tears running out of the corners of his eyes and down his cheeks. "You've really got great spit," he said. And Dale dug his knees into his flank, as if he were urging a horse to greater speed. "You went along with the rest of us that night we burned down his barn, and I never said anything about that."

"Is that what you're afraid of?"

"I'm not afraid of anything," Dale said. "I know what you're thinking about. But I don't feel one damn bit guilty. I was there and I saw it happen. I even heard the last thing he ever said. He said, 'Why is the road here so soft?' And then he died. And that's all there was to it, it's all over, I put all of that behind me. What's over is over."

"Not as far as I'm concerned," Paul said. "And now I wish you'd get off me so I could wipe my face."

Obediently, Dale got up, stood over Paul, who took out his handkerchief and patted his face with it. "It even hurts to smile," Paul said. Dale grunted. "But you know, I wonder," Paul went on, "why is the beach here so soft?"

And Dale spat on him again, and he shouted, "Go to hell! You rotten bastard, go to hell!" And he ran back to the hotel.

Paul stretched out on the sand, lost sight of the retreating figure. His mouth was still bleeding; he rolled onto his side and in the moonlight could see the blood fall and soak into the cool sand, like wine on a tablecloth. The wind

162

came in from the sea and the waves rolled on, applauding themselves *I am strangely content* on his back again he tried for a time to count the number of stars in the Big Dipper, but he fell asleep before he could finish.

"It's after five now," Laura said, glancing at her wrist watch. The leaves cracked in the wind; some of the trees were already bare. "My, it gets dark early now, doesn't it?"

Dorothy Mae stepped off the walk and stood by a naked mountain ash; she pulled a cluster of orange berries from the tree. "These are poison," she said. "Still, I've heard that the birds eat them. I wonder why that is."

"Maybe they've built up a tolerance to the poison," Alex said.

"What's that?" Dorothy Mae asked.

"Tolerance? Sort of a resistance, like taking very small amounts of poison so that your body can get used to it, and then when you take larger doses your body is accustomed to it and knows how to handle it. I guess that's more or less the way it is."

She tossed the berries aside, headed for the recreation building, across the lawn, ploughing through the crisp leaves. Alex and Laura caught up to her and walked one on either side. "How's Tony?" she asked.

"He's fine," Alex said.

"How's his arm?" She asked.

"Fine, I guess," Alex said.

"Did he tell you about it?"

"He showed me," Alex said. "But I see him around, he looks all right, I suppose it's healed."

"I'm not sorry," she said. "Not really."

"That's up to you," he said.

"I could've killed," she said. "Did he tell you that?"

"Yes, he told me that."

"Did he ask you to come up here?"

"Yes, it was his idea," he said.

"Why couldn't he come himself?" she asked.

"Maybe he didn't know what to say," Alex said.

Now they could see inside. In the main recreation room, where Alex and Laura had met Dorothy Mae, there were people dancing: standing apart, undulating. But one couple, apparently quite out of step with the music, or impervious to it, or both, were bound closely together, glided in what seemed to be a waltz tempo. As they drew closer, they could see that it was Miss Parker and a pimply young man hardly into his twenties. "Do you like to dance?" Alex asked.

"I don't know how," she said. "At least not that way."

"They're not all doing it that way, though." Alex pointed to the sedately twirling couple, Miss Parker and her partner.

"Yes," she said. "I can dance that way. I can dance the polka too. And the schottische. Old-time music they used to call it. They don't play it too much anymore."

They entered the building; Alex held the door for the two women. Then he took the notebook from the yielding Dorothy Mae and gave it to Laura to hold. "Now we'll dance," he said, and he took Dorothy Mae's hand and led her into the room. The portable phonograph was turned as loud as the volume control would permit; there was only one record on the turntable, playing and replaying, Chuck Berry's *Maybelline*, about a Cadillac and a Ford racing, a two dollar bill, and Maybelline who couldn't be true. She put her hand on his shoulder, he put his arm around her waist—"I'm really a very poor dancer," he said.

She nodded, "So am I."

"We'll have to watch how she does it," he said, pointing toward Miss Parker.

The record finished, the arm clicked up and over and back again; the music began, and they pushed off: a-one-and-a-two-and-back-and-one-and-two-and-back-and-one-and-two-and-back. They danced: a beat behind the music, still closer to the beat than Miss Parker and her friend. They danced, not lightly, haltingly, uncertainly, neither of them leading. Dorothy Mae concentrated, nibbled her lip. He leaned toward her, to speak into her ear, "Tony asked me to come," he said. She nodded. "He asked me . . . ." but then the music stopped, all the dancers stopped, and they waited for the arm to lift up and return again to the beginning. The music began and they danced, more surely this time. "He asked me. . . ." He was leading now, she followed, not yet gracefully, but assenting to the beat of the music. "He asked me to ask you," Alex said, speaking into her ear over the pulsing of the music, "if you would forgive him." She danced on, followed him, looked into his eyes. She nodded Yes.

And the music stopped, just barely stopped, before Miss Parker came over with her young man, whom she introduced to Dorothy Mae. "This is Herbie," she said. "From St. Paul. He has beautiful dreams, dear." Herbie cut in; he put his arm around Dorothy Mae's waist, she put her hand on his shoulder, the music began, and they danced. "And you, dear?" Miss Parker asked. Alex nodded Yes. And off he danced with Miss Parker. "I'll bet you have lots and lots of dreams, dear," she said. "Yes," Alex said. He nodded. And they danced.

Type, 11 on 13 Baskerville
Display, Optima
Paper, "R" Antique